OF BOOKS AND MAGES

OF BOOKS AND MAGES

A SPOKEN MAGE NOVELLA

MELANIE CELLIER

THE SPOKEN MAGE BOOK 5.5

Luminant Publications
PO Box 305
Greenacres, South Australia 5086

melanie@melaniecellier.com
http://www.melaniecellier.com

Cover Design by Karri Klawiter
Editing by Mary Novak
Proofreading by James Packer
Map Illustration by Rebecca E Paavo

For Priya,
the first to sit down with me and discuss what a world of written power might look like. Thank you for still being interested a decade later.

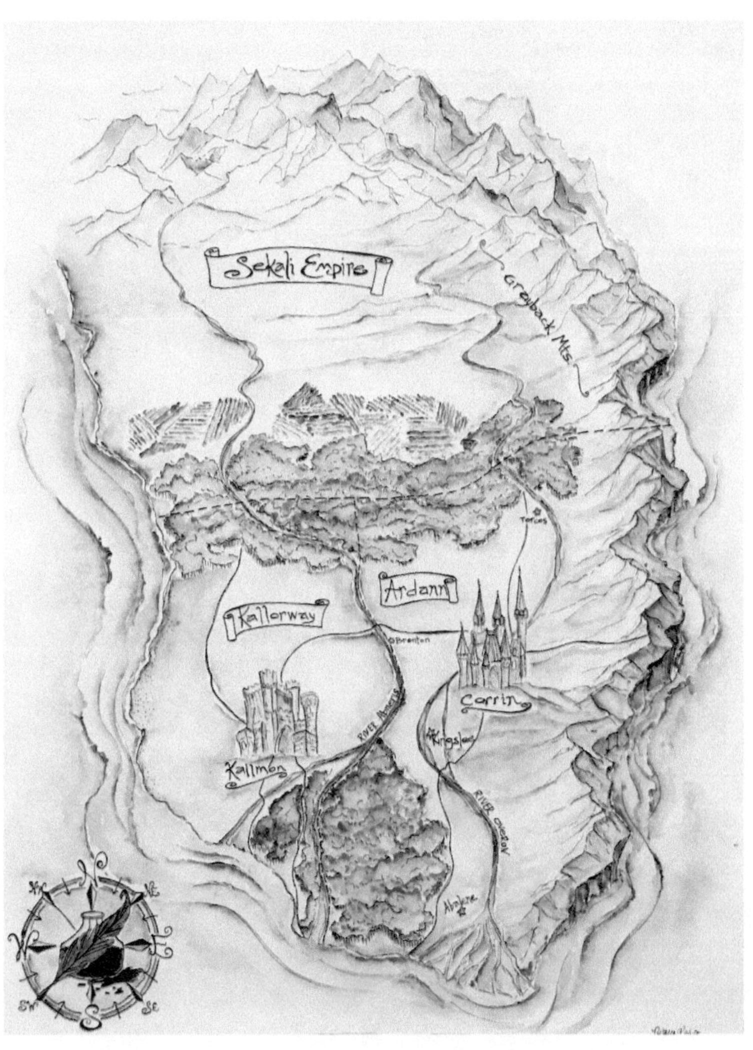

Sekali Empire
Greyback Mts.
Ardann
Kallorway
Torcs
Brenton
Corrin
Kallmor
RIVER Abuella
Kingslee
RIVER Chatov
Mistere
N
NE
NW
E
W
SW
S
SE

CHAPTER 1

I hurried along the side street toward home. I had lingered in the study hall longer than intended, and the day was drawing toward its close, despite the summer light that still lingered in the air. If I didn't hurry, I would be late for the evening meal, and no excuse would pacify my mother if I was late for my own birthday celebration.

Eighteen. The number lingered in my mind, a sour note on what should have been a joyful day. Most people rejoiced at turning eighteen and entering full adulthood. But for me, the age loomed over me like a storm cloud.

At thirteen years old, when they announced the opening of advanced schools for commonborns, eighteen had seemed unimaginably far away. I had already finished ordinary schooling at age ten, but my apprenticeship in my parents' small business hadn't interested me the way it did my older brothers. I wanted more schooling, and the initial euphoric rush of sealing ceremonies, followed by the announcement of advanced schools, had promised to make my wildest dreams into reality.

I had rushed to attend the testing that would allow already graduated youth to return to school and extend their schooling as far as eighteen. But I had been certain I would be chosen for sealing long before then. So many sealing ceremonies had already been held to give the chosen commonborn access to written words, and I knew I would be part of a ceremony soon. I wouldn't be in school for another five years.

And yet eighteen had arrived, and I was still in the advanced school—the oldest remaining student.

Not that all those who started with me in the initial rush of excitement had been sealed, of course. After the first wave, the number of sealing ceremonies dwindled drastically. Among mages, only criminals and those who failed the Mage Academy had their access to power sealed—along with the fortunate commonborns who joined them inside their sealing ceremony, thus ensuring they could safely write without releasing uncontrolled power. Once the prisons were emptied, the number of ceremonies were few and far between. I should have foreseen it, of course, but I was too caught up in the new possibilities for my future.

With so few opportunities for advanced students to be sealed, most of my peers had dropped away, entering apprenticeships or taking up jobs as they lost hope of ever being selected. And those who had been chosen had also left—bound for the teaching college or the Royal University and the prestigious positions that would come after.

In my time at school, two older students, once sealed,

had chosen the college and a future as a teacher in one of the kingdom's many commonborn schools. The rest had joined the commonborn class at the Royal University for a future as an official or academic. Not that sealing required you to take either option. A Robart boy two years below me, who often boasted of soon being selected, intended to take up a position with his wealthy commonborn merchant family where he would be trained extensively on the job.

My choice was the Royal University, and I had been dreaming of it for five years. Eighteen and still at school because I couldn't let go of my hope.

You're too stubborn, Aria. I could hear my mother's exasperated voice in my head, and for the first time, the words cracked a fault line in my optimism.

In a single short week, I would officially finish my schooling. My opportunities for selection had narrowed to one last desperate possibility.

I gritted my teeth and increased my speed. There was still hope. Our final test was only three days away, and I would keep studying hard until the last moment. Rumors claimed that the crop of graduating mages this year was strong, but there was still the chance one of them would fail the Mage Academy. And with just one failure would come my chance for a future—mine and so many other commonborns.

And that was why I had remained in the study hall so late, even on my birthday. If there was a chance for commonborns to be included in the sealing ceremony of a failed mage trainee, only the top student from our school would be sent. And this year I wasn't allowing anything to come between myself and first place.

My steps faltered as a noise caught my ears. I turned toward a side alley, my mind struggling to identify the sound that had tripped my steps. I usually tuned out the noise of the city. Corrin, capital of Ardann, was a large and bustling place full of any number of sounds, both day and night.

And yet my ear caught on this one, my body halting in response. Glancing around, I realized I was alone on the street. A chill crept across my scalp. My eyes flicked again toward the dark alley as I willed my feet to resume moving, carrying me toward home. My body remained stationary, however, my natural curiosity warring with my instinctive fear.

My thoughts had caught up with my subconscious and identified the sound I had heard—the edge of a blade drawn along stone. It was a chilling sound, which was why it was the sound effect of choice for every child telling the tale of the Shrouded Mage. The unknown mage, who had stalked the backstreets of Corrin for almost a year looking for commonborn prey, was a favorite topic among those looking to scare their younger siblings and friends.

But the murderer currently being hunted by the entire law enforcement discipline wouldn't actually go around dulling his blade for no reason. I wasn't even sure he used a knife at all. Just because stories of him always included that sound didn't mean it signified his presence.

You're going to get yourself murdered! Running around the city at all hours of the day and night! My mother's voice sounded in my head again.

But despite the taut bowstring of my nerves, I didn't believe her words any more now than I had at the time. Statistically speaking, the chance of my ending up as the Shrouded Mage's next victim was vanishingly small—especially given all his (or her) victims so far had been men.

My nerves hummed anyway.

My straining ears caught on new sounds, almost hidden beneath the noise of the city. But the thump of flesh striking flesh was unmistakable, along with the gasps and pants that indicated a desperate struggle.

A new thought flashed into my mind. What if it was, indeed, the Shrouded Mage, and he was in the middle of attacking his next target?

I knew what my mother would say. She would tell me to use the killer's distraction to escape. But my feet were already carrying me toward the alley's entrance.

A pile of crates stood a few feet back from the street, blocking my view into the alley beyond. I peered cautiously around them and gasped.

Rather than a single attacker, his face masked and obscured by a hood, and a single victim, four figures struggled back and forth. A splatter of blood already colored one of the stone walls. I wasn't witness to the next Shrouded Mage killing, but I had stumbled on three ruffians assaulting a lone young man.

A sword rested against one wall of the alley where it must have been kicked during the conflict—presumably the source of the sound that had first caught my ears. One of the attackers hung back, one hand clutching his shoulder, red welling between his fingers. But he remained on his feet, calling encouragement to the other two who fought their opponent hand to hand, their blows and blocks falling so fast I could barely follow them.

My mother's shouts to flee rang as loudly in my ears as if she'd actually spoken them, but the victim's eyes caught on mine for the briefest second, and the expression on his face compelled me to act. Despite being alone against three attackers, he fought with desperation and skill, grim determination underlined by unexpected hopelessness, as if he had no expectation of assistance or rescue.

I launched myself into the pile of empty crates with a battle cry. It was a fearsome sound, if I said so myself, honed from years of mock battles with my four brothers.

The teetering pile exploded away from me, crates crashing in all directions and consuming the four figures inside the alley. The sound of battle broke off, replaced with mingled shouts of surprise and pain.

It had been an inspired move, taking full advantage of the element of surprise. Unfortunately, my brilliance ended there. My own body fell into the alley along with the crates, joining the chaos of flailing limbs and splintering wood.

I struggled to regain my footing, falling twice and rolling across the ground before I managed to find my balance. My right arm fell against a splintered crate, a jagged piece of wood piercing it deeply.

I shouted at the pain, but the crate had already snapped, leaving only a small length of wood still speared into my arm. I hissed and reached for it before remembering the ruffians. Seizing up a second jagged length of broken wood and holding it like a stake, I scrambled to my feet and spun around, looking for an opponent.

Even with my assistance, we were still outnumbered three to two. And I wasn't sure I counted for much given the size of the ruffians and my lack of combat training.

My eyes swept the narrow confines of the alley, my teeth clenched against the pain in my arm. But astonishment overtook my determination. All four of the men had also regained their feet, but instead of rejoining battle, the ruffians were fleeing the alley, their shouts already receding as they reached its entrance. Before my wide eyes, the three of them disappeared into the street beyond, the last throwing a terrified look over his shoulder.

"I had no idea I was so fearsome," I said, still trying to block out the pain.

My remaining companion laughed. "You certainly make an impression. For a moment, I thought we were being attacked by a horde."

I managed a grin. "Where size is lacking, you must make up for it with noise."

"I'll remember that for the future." His voice held a chuckle, and he stepped toward me. "I'm Zakary, by the way."

"I'm Aria."

His smile died as he got a proper look at me, his eyes fastening on the spear of jagged wood protruding from my arm. I regarded him back curiously, noting that he was in even worse shape.

He wore simple brown leather and a shirt that must once have been white. Dirt and blood now streaked it, and one of his arms hung limply at his side.

I winced. "That looks broken."

He nodded confirmation, holding up the other hand.

"And at least one of these fingers, I think." His knuckles were spotted with blood, and the hand was already beginning to swell.

I swallowed, glad that the possession of four brothers had discouraged any tendency toward squeamishness.

"We're a fair way from any of the healing clinics," I gasped, fighting a fresh wave of pain from my arm. "So we better get moving. Otherwise one of us is going to collapse before we get there." I grimaced. "And I hope those men didn't succeed in taking your coin because I don't have any."

I fixed him with a challenging stare in case he was thinking of telling me to pay for myself. I had been injured saving him, so the least he could do was patch me up enough to make it home. I wouldn't expect him to pay for a full healing, but I needed something or I was going to faint.

I started slowly toward the alley mouth, grimacing at my lack of strength. What would happen if we both collapsed short of the healing clinic? Maybe we should head for my house instead—it was much closer, and once we reached it, my father could fetch a cart to carry us there.

Glancing back over my shoulder, I frowned. Zakary hadn't moved. Instead, he appeared to be trying to reach inside his vest. The attempted movement made him hiss and pull back his injured hand.

I stomped back over to him. "What in the kingdom are you doing?" I shook my head. "Are you trying to make those fingers worse?"

He sighed. "Both arms! It's really too bad." He threw a quick look up and down the alley—still deserted but for the two of us—and lowered his voice. "If you could just reach in and retrieve them for me, I don't see how it could do any harm."

I stared at him. Had he taken a blow to the head as well?

"Obviously I won't say anything to anyone," he said. "You just have to slide your hand in between the vest and my shirt. Skip the first internal pocket—it's the second one we want."

"The *second* internal pocket?" Maybe he had a history of blows to the head. How many internal pockets did one person need?

He swayed, his face draining of still more color, and I sighed. Maybe if I humored him and retrieved whatever he was after, we could finally get moving toward the healers. I clearly couldn't leave him here on his own with two useless arms. He'd probably collapse and die on the spot, after all my hard work to save him.

At least I didn't have to worry about the awkward closeness the move would require. He clearly wasn't in a fit state to do me or anyone else any harm.

Sighing, I carefully slid my hand beneath his vest. His shirt still lay between my fingers and the skin of his chest, but warmth flared in my cheeks anyway. Despite my best efforts, it was impossible not to feel the smooth muscles of his chest. Even dirty and blood-stained, he was undeniably attractive. I guessed him to be a couple of years older than me, too. If he'd been a student in my class, I would have developed a crush on our first day.

My fingers slid past one pocket, my breath catching as I heard a familiar rustle. Did he have paper hidden beneath his clothes?

I nearly drew my hand back out empty, but my fingers had already found the second pocket, and they grasped instinctively on the collection of tiny tubes there. Whipping my hand back out, I dropped the retrieved items as if scalded, and backed away, eyes wide. In the open, I could see that the tubes were small, tightly rolled strips of parchment.

"Is that writing?" I took another step back as I looked at the clear skin of his wrists. Peering up and down the alley, I unthinkingly mirrored his earlier movement. Now I knew the reason for his surreptitious look. "Are you trying to get me arrested by the Grays?"

Zakary's attention was on the rolls of parchment, and he barely seemed to hear my words.

"Did you have to drop them? It's filthy down there." He sighed and slowly lowered himself into a crouch. "But I suppose a bit of dirt won't mar their power."

Power? I sucked in a breath at the word, several things becoming clear. Those scraps of paper weren't forbidden writing—they were *compositions*. I had been looking for signs that he was sealed, and therefore allowed to read and write, but Zakary wasn't a commonborn at all. He was a mage.

CHAPTER 2

No wonder he had so many internal pockets. It made sense that mages would want to keep their compositions on their person, and they would need some way to organize them and quickly access the right ones.

Zackary sucked in a pained breath as he retrieved one of the compositions in his two least injured fingers. He shook it out enough to get a glimpse of the words written on the parchment. I quickly averted my face, making it obvious I wasn't trying to spy on the writing. He didn't seem to notice either way, though.

"Yes, this one to start with," he muttered, only to pause and look at me. "Which one of us is worse off?" I opened my mouth to say it was definitely him, but he had already continued speaking. "Never mind that. You saved me."

Lifting the coiled rectangle of parchment to his mouth, he gripped it between his teeth and pulled, ripping it in half. He let the halves drift to the ground, flicking his few working fingers in my direction.

The pain lifted instantly, shock waves of relief rolling through me. The dizziness ebbed along with it, so I peered at my arm. Surely he hadn't healed me?

The jagged wood still remained in place, untouched. But now that the pain was gone, I could absorb that it was bleeding only sluggishly, the wood plugging the hole it had created. It was the pain, not blood loss, that had pushed me near collapse.

I looked up in time to see Zakary tear a second roll of parchment, this time flicking his fingers at himself. The lines on his face instantly eased and his shoulders relaxed.

"That is a great deal better." He grinned at me, and despite everything, I grinned back. Sudden relief from intense pain was a heady feeling.

"You're a mage," I said somewhat foolishly, and he nodded.

"I am." He crouched back down to scoop up the remaining rolls of parchment, his movements still clumsy and awkward. "So there's no need to report me to the Grays for illicit reading."

He shot me a smile, but I didn't smile back. As a mage-born, he had been born with the bloodline to control power, so he had never been at risk from the gray-robed mages of the seekers. The discipline that hunted down anyone learning to read illegally was only a threat to unsealed commonborn—the ones who might accidentally blow ourselves up if we ever tried to write, taking a whole chunk of the city with us. Zakary had never been forbidden access to the written word as I had always been.

My eyes lingered hungrily on the parchment in his hands. I had worked hard for five years to win the right to access words, and yet that dream was still as far away as ever.

He looked painstakingly through the parchments that remained whole, finally choosing one and lifting it to his teeth to tear it. As I watched, fascinated, his limp arm straightened, and he flexed the fingers of the opposite hand, his grip on the remaining parchments shifting and strengthening.

"You healed yourself?" I gasped at him as he swung both arms, testing them.

He nodded, but his expression was apologetic. "I'm sorry I can't do the same for you. My injuries were more immediately debilitating, but they were just clean breaks. Whereas your situation is more complicated." He grimaced. "I'd have to start by pulling that wood out for one, and that might cause a lot of bleeding. If I messed up the healing..." He sighed. "I should have taken more healing classes."

I shook my head. I had no doubt the compositions he'd already used were incredibly valuable. He must have written them himself, perhaps in his days at the Royal Academy.

I eyed him again. He wasn't wearing a white trainee's robe, which meant he had to be older than I'd first imagined. Now that my mind wasn't clouded by pain, I had so many questions. What was he doing in this part of the city?

The answer to that question was obvious, though. He had to be a weak mage from one of the minor families. The type who was just strong enough to pass the Academy and avoid having his power sealed, but who wasn't strong enough to be accepted to a mage discipline. Mages like that sometimes chose to make a living by either tutoring commonborn—reading aloud the words we couldn't read ourselves—or selling compositions to those commonborn rich enough to buy them. The compositions I'd retrieved for him hadn't been secured shut and color-coded, though, so presumably he sold to sealed commonborn only.

The loss of three healing compositions represented a significant loss of income. How difficult had they been for him to make? He'd probably prostrated himself for a day or more to compose the one for breaks.

And he'd used the first of his compositions on me. I smiled at him, softened. But a fresh thought jolted through me, making me stiffen. I'd nearly forgotten it was my birthday.

"You've taken the pain away, which is the main thing," I said hurriedly. "Now I have the strength to get home."

"Home?" He stepped toward me, looking alarmed. "You have a piece of wood sticking out of your arm! You can't just go home."

I laughed. "If I don't go home my mother will kill me, and then any healing compositions used on me will have been wasted."

"Your own mother isn't going to kill you for getting a necessary healing." He regarded me suspiciously, as if he suspected some ulterior motive.

"You haven't met my mother." I grinned and shook my head. "She's probably already furious that I'm late, and she'd be even more furious if I went to a healing clinic without consulting her first. She used to be a healing assistant before she joined my father's business, and she's always taken care of our illnesses and injuries. Plus, it's my birthday today." A small swell of the earlier missing pride hit me unexpectedly. "I'm eighteen today, and she's planned a special meal."

"It's your birthday!" Zakary sounded more shocked than the occasion warranted. "And you were on your way to your own party?" He shook his head. "But you stopped to help me anyway. My gratitude has doubled. Thank you. And happy birthday."

Maybe I was still a little out of my mind from the pain relief because I leaned forward and said conversationally, "I thought you might be the Shrouded Mage."

"The Shrouded Ma…" Zakary blinked. "Oh! You mean the Shrouded Killer."

I refrained from rolling my eyes, but only barely. So the mages had a different name for him. The Reds had used their law enforcement compositions to prove the killer was a mage, but of course the mageborn wouldn't want to acknowledge that fact every time they referred to the criminal.

Zakary blinked at me several more times as he absorbed my meaning. "You thought I was an infamous killer who stalks the lower city for his victims, and you therefore ran *toward* me."

"I was going to run away," I said, "but then I heard the sounds of a struggle. I was running toward the victim, not the killer."

"A meaningless distinction if they were locked in a struggle at the time," he said dryly, but he looked impressed.

My insides warmed, my chest tightening in response to the warmth of admiration in his eyes.

"Thankfully for both of us, they were just ordinary thieves," I said, aware that the Shrouded Mage wouldn't have been run off so easily.

Zakary grimaced. "I might have had a better chance against one mage than three commonborn, actually. I didn't think I would be so easily overcome, but I'm not used to fighting so many at once. They kept me too busy to retrieve a composition in the first few seconds, and then…" He gestured toward the arm that had been broken.

I shook my head, unconvinced. "If the Shrouded Mage was an easy target, law enforcement wouldn't still be hunting him after all this time." I sighed, hating the thought of the menace who was casting a shadow over the lower city. "If you ask me, you were extremely fortunate." I cast an eye over him, trying to picture him without the dirt and blood. "You're a good fit for the kind of victims he targets."

Zakary's eyes lit up. "You think so?"

I stared at him. Did he have a death wish? He'd been too quick to heal himself for that to make any sense.

I wanted to linger and question him further. I'd never had a conversation this long with a mage before. But I could feel a clock ticking in my head. My guests would have already arrived. I took a step backward toward the mouth of the alley.

"Those three definitely weren't the Shrouded Killer," Zakary continued. "The law enforcement mages have already established that he works alone. These ones were just copycats."

Once again his speech patterns marked him as a mage. Among the commonborn, we just called law enforcement the Reds, not bothering with their official title. His words kept broadcasting that he was out of his element, so it was no wonder he'd gotten into trouble—wandering the streets of the lower city without a single clue.

But his conclusion interested me. "What do you mean by copycats?" I could afford to linger for another minute or two.

Zakary's mouth twisted. "They wouldn't be the first, unfortunately. Once the actions of a repeat criminal become known, some people see a terrible sort of opportunity. They think that if they make their crime match the shrouded killings closely enough, then law enforcement will assume it was the Shrouded Killer and not come after them."

My mouth fell open, anger filling me. "But that's awful!"

He gave a wry smile. "Yes. But I'm guessing people who are willing to kill don't have a lot of scruples."

I screwed up my nose, but I couldn't deny his logic. "It's a good thing I came along when I did."

I edged another step backward.

"You'll at least let me walk you to your home?" He looked perturbed. "What if my pain composition doesn't last long enough, and you end up collapsing partway there? You were injured saving me, and I can't just walk away without being sure you're going to be all right."

I couldn't help another flood of warmth at his genuine concern, but I couldn't arrive home not only injured, but with a mage in tow. My family were going to be shocked enough, but they would be furious if they grasped the full extent of my reckless actions.

"That's all right," I said hurriedly. "It isn't far."

I took yet another step toward the freedom of the street.

"Wait!" Zakary leaped forward and grasped at my sleeve. "I can't just let you walk off with a piece of wood sticking out of your arm!"

I pulled away instinctively, and my already damaged shirt tore further, sending a small item tumbling to the ground. I gasped and lunged for it, but my injured arm hampered my movements, and Zakary got there first.

The apologies on his lips died as he took in what he held in his hands. He looked up at me slowly, and I took another step back. But I couldn't actually flee. Not while he was still holding the folded and sealed parchment.

Leaping forward, Zakary clamped an iron hand around my good forearm, pulling it forward so he could examine my wrist. It was conspicuously clear of the intricate pattern of dark skin pigmentation that would have marked me as sealed.

I wasn't sealed, and we both knew it. And that made the letter in his hand a serious crime. The sides of the alley caved in on me, extinguishing the last ember of hope I had been clinging to so desperately.

CHAPTER 3

"*Y*ou aren't sealed." Zakary's voice held as much steel as the hand that still gripped my arm. "What are you doing with writing?"

"It isn't mine," I gasped out, my whole body frozen.

"You know that doesn't matter," he growled. "Unsealed commonborn are not permitted words."

Terror filled me, more potent than what I had felt during the attack. It strengthened my spine and lent fire to my voice. I would have to be more brazen than I had ever been before if I had any hope of salvaging my future.

"I just saved your life. Are you telling me you're going to hand me over to the Grays for a single sealed letter?"

His grip on my arm didn't loosen, but his posture softened, his face twisting. Gratitude and personal obligation warred with his ingrained duty.

"Who taught you to read?" he asked. "And who has been foolhardy enough to write you a letter?"

He glanced down at the sealed missive, anger in his eyes although I wasn't sure if it was directed at me or the letter's unknown author. He must have wanted to break it open and look for a signature, but he couldn't easily do so without relinquishing his hold on me.

At least he wasn't making any attempt to drag me away. I had an opening, and I needed to push until it turned into a path forward.

"You don't have to quote lectures at me about reading leading to writing," I said with as much indignation as I could muster. "In my ten years of study, I've never attempted to read, not even once. I wouldn't put my dreams and future at risk so foolishly."

Both his brows shot up. "Excuse me if I find that a little hard to believe, given this." He shook the letter slightly.

My heart beat fast, but I forced myself to meet his eyes. "You can see it has a seal. It isn't for me, and I have no intention of reading it."

"Just carrying it with you is a very serious crime. If you're still studying, you must be hoping to win a place in a sealing ceremony. Having this in your possession alone means you would never be chosen—and worse consequences besides."

"Only if someone catches me with it," I said, but the words fell dully onto the cobblestones between us, my summoned fire sputtering and dying. Someone *had* caught me with it.

But as my hope died away, some of Zakary's ire seemed to die with it. He looked between the folded letter and me, curiosity in his eyes.

"If the letter isn't for you—if it's true you can't even read—why would you risk carrying it with you?"

I bit my lip. "I have to stay on my teacher's good side," I blurted out. "There's another Robart two years below me."

He leaned back a little, his grip slackening and his brow creased. "What?"

I sighed. "I know you're a mage, but even you must have heard of the Robarts. They may be commonborn, but they're a powerful merchant family."

"Of course I've heard of them. But what do they have to do with this?"

I groaned. "Most of them live in this section of the city."

"Is your teacher a Robart, then?" Zakary frowned. "And he gave you this? I still don't understand."

"No, he isn't a Robart." My voice dropped to a mutter. "He just wishes he was." I took one look at Zakary's confused expression and sighed again.

If it was going to make sense to him, I needed to tell him the whole story. It wasn't something I liked to talk about, but I would tell Zakary my deepest childhood secrets if there was any chance they would extricate me from the situation.

They wouldn't, of course. But if I could make him understand my position, maybe this tale could.

"I've been top of the class for the last four years," I told him flatly, unable to muster any pride since the vast effort had so far gained me nothing. "The other students didn't even resent me for it—much—since they knew I worked twice as hard as anyone else."

"And yet..." Zakary's eyes dropped to my unmarked wrist.

"You must know there haven't been many sealing cere-monies in the last few years." I tried to squash the defensive note in my voice. "There were several in my first year at the school, when I was still too young, but in the last four there has only been one."

Zakary swallowed and nodded, unease in his face. "Two years ago. When a trainee failed the Academy."

For a moment I was distracted by the incongruity of his emotion until it hit me once again how differently he saw the world. In the lower city, among the commonborn, an Academy failure was a matter of excitement—even rejoicing. Among the mages, it must be something both feared and dreaded.

"Yes, that's the one," I said, my voice softer. "The office for the management of sealed affairs requested a name from every school in the kingdom. Just one name. Each school was supposed to nominate their top student among those sixteen and older."

"And that was you." He watched my face intently, caught in my story as I had hoped.

"It was." My voice held a fierce note despite myself. "It should have been me. My teacher knew it. Everyone knew it."

"So what happened?" Zakary's grip had slackened, although he didn't entirely let go, the warm circle of his fingers now soft against my skin.

"We had a second Robart among us back then—my closest friend at the school, Gina. We were the same age, and she was great fun, but she didn't have the same dedication to her studies as I did. She didn't want it as badly." A lump formed in the back of my throat, and I pushed it away. "She was the one to join me whenever I emerged from my studying to have a moment of fun."

"Fun." Zakary's voice held the ghost of a chuckle, giving me a surge of hope. "Things like catapulting yourself into piles of crates and leaping on armed attackers? That sort of fun?"

I managed a grin. "You should chat with my mother some time. She's always bemoaning that such a diligent student can also be so wild and reckless. But she doesn't understand how wearing it gets, acting with control and discipline all the time. Sometimes I have to rebel and do something wild or I might explode."

Zakary's eyes dropped to the letter in his hand, and his amusement dimmed. "So you did something reckless and got yourself overlooked two years ago?"

"No!"

I almost wished I had. If it had been my fault I wasn't chosen, maybe it would have been easier to bear.

"I wasn't reckless, I just got sick. Not even badly sick. I just got a poorly timed summer cold."

Zakary frowned. "What difference did that make?"

"All the difference in the kingdom." I drew a deep breath as I reached the painful part of the story. "My head was so heavy and foggy for the last test of the year that I didn't perform to my usual standard. Gina, on the other hand, did unusually well. She usually placed in the middle of the class, but she came first that time. I thought she must have studied extra hard and even congratulated her on her success."

I dwelt darkly on that thought for a moment before forcing my mind onward.

"Then the news came about the failure of the mage trainee. I was so elated that I sprinted all the way to school, needing official confirmation that our teacher had been asked to nominate someone for the sealing." My voice faltered at the memory of the devastation that had so taken me by surprise.

"You said Gina is a Robart." Zakary said the words with grim understanding, proving the quickness of his mind.

I nodded miserably. "The teachers are supposed to nominate their top student, and everyone knew that was me. But that last test gave him the excuse he needed to choose Gina instead."

"And you said she studied extra hard for that one test." Zakary spoke the words levelly, but I caught a spark in his eyes.

I nodded again. "It's obvious in retrospect. The Robarts are influential enough to know what's happening among the mages. They must have known a failure was likely. I honestly thought Gina was my friend, but…"

"But she seized her chance when it came." His voice turned gentle.

"She never even returned to the school. I haven't seen her since."

Zakary winced, and I pushed away the old pain. I had to focus on what was happening now if I wanted to avoid an even more devastating blow to my future than Gina's betrayal.

"From that experience, I learned that it's not enough to be top of the class. I need to be in the teacher's goodwill as well. He received many marks of favor from the Robarts after Gina was sealed, and I know he has expectations of transferring to a position in their company in the next couple of years. But that's given me an opening. He's grown increasingly resentful of the demands of his teaching role, and he's always complaining about not having enough time. So I do him small favors whenever I can, like delivering a letter for him."

"This isn't a small favor!" Zakary let me go at last, and the sudden lack of contact left me feeling unmoored. I rubbed my palm against the filthy material of my clothes.

"He must know he could get in as much trouble as you!" Zakary strode a few paces away and then wheeled to come back. "What's his name?"

I shook my head rapidly. "I'm not saying."

He looked down at the letter in his hands, and I lunged forward, managing to take him by surprise and seize it back. "No, please. Don't!"

We stood, eyes locked, my breath coming in ragged gasps.

"Please," I whispered softly.

Zakary's shoulders slumped as he rubbed a hand over his face and groaned. "You did save my life." He looked at the letter in my hand with uncertainty before his eyes rose to my face. "You really can't read? You weren't going to open it?"

I nodded fervently, trying to look earnest and trustworthy. "I do not want to turn into a giant fireball."

He blew out a long breath. "My friends would say I'm a fool for letting myself get dragged into this—I could end up in trouble with the seekers myself…" He sighed. "But what am I going to do? Drag you down to their headquarters and hand you in while you still have a spear of wood sticking out of your arm from saving my life?"

I rose onto the balls of my feet, the kernel of hope

unfurling inside me. I had gotten myself into a dangerous mess, but apparently I was going to slip out of it again by the thinnest of margins.

"Thank you! And you really don't need to worry about me reading. I'm not doing any harm, I'm truly not."

Zakary stepped close to me again, and for one unthinking moment I was conscious only of the warmth he sparked inside me. Then he stretched out his hand and snatched back the letter.

I gaped at him. "But you just said—"

"I said I wouldn't turn you in. But I also said we could all land in trouble for this. I'm not going to send you off to parade around the city with written words tucked in your shirt."

My face flushed, this time with fear and anger. The school year wasn't quite over, so there was still the slim possibility that a sealing ceremony would be announced before I was forced to graduate. But if I lost Teacher Wendell's letter, he would never choose me. My last chance would be truly gone.

Zakary sighed, his eyes on my face. "Don't worry. I'll make sure it gets to its intended recipient. You wouldn't be able to read it, but her name is on the outside."

I stiffened. If I was going down, I would willingly take Teacher Wendell with me. He had wronged me terribly two years ago, and I was well aware he had continued to do so with every request for me to deliver a letter since. He had grown overconfident since coming into the Robarts' sphere, convinced there was no chance anyone would discover his little shortcut.

But Faylee was another matter. She might be a Robart,

but she wasn't anything like Gina or my teacher. In fact, I already suspected Teacher Wendell had misjudged when he used me to deliver a letter to her. He had done so because he heard she was going to be at my birthday meal that night, but I didn't think she was going to be happy about discovering he'd been using me as a messenger. Faylee was known for being blunt, and while she wouldn't turn us in, neither would she spare either of our feelings when she upbraided us both for fools.

"Don't worry," Zakary said, apparently reading my reaction with ease. "It wasn't Faylee who gave you the letter. As far as I'm aware, she's done no wrong here. Yet. I would like a word with her, though."

Despite the apparent reassurance of the start of his speech, his final line filled me with foreboding. But I also noted the way he said her name.

"You know Faylee?" I looked hopefully at him. Surely he wouldn't want to bring any harm down on her if he knew her.

"In person, no. But everyone has heard of Faylee."

I grinned. Faylee had been sealed in the first wave of ceremonies and had to be the most famous commonborn in Ardann—and she was my friend.

I wasn't foolish enough to think it was due to any great virtue on my part. I had always known the young woman offered me her mentorship because she knew the truth of what her family had done to me. Unlike other Robarts, she was ashamed of their family's dishonest dealing. But now that we had gotten to know each other, I sometimes thought she genuinely liked me and didn't only offer friendship out of obligation.

"I'll see the letter safely where it belongs." Zakary stowed it in one of his endless internal pockets.

I watched it disappear with reluctance, but I was exceedingly fortunate if I escaped this lightly. If Zakary was true to his word, I only had to dread what Faylee would say to me after his visit. Would she be disgusted enough to drop our connection as Gina had once done?

The thought brought me pain—especially since it would be a result of my own foolish choices if she did. I shouldn't have let my dreams lead me into such risky action.

"I need to get home," I said shakily, expecting Zakary to protest again.

He didn't.

Swallowing, I murmured a final thank you and hurried out into the street, cradling my injured arm against my chest. The discovery of the letter had changed his attitude toward me completely, but I had no right to feel disappointed after what he had discovered.

Of course, if I'd been sealed two years ago, everything would have been different. I could have carried as many letters as I wished openly and with pride. And Zakary wouldn't have looked at me as if—

I broke off my thoughts with a shaky laugh, turning into my street with a shake of my head. The blood loss—minor as it was—must have been affecting me after all. Sealed or not made little difference. Zakary was a mage, and even a minor mage was on an entirely different social level from a commonborn. He had been grateful to me for saving his life, but his interest ended there and my circumstances had nothing to do with it.

A lancing pain hit me as I hurried through my front door, making me stumble. More pain followed in its wake until I was awash with it.

Zakary's pain relief composition had run out of power, just as he had feared. Workings like that were usually designed to cover the short time that it took to diagnose the issue and work a proper healing composition, as Zakary had done for himself.

"Aria!" My second oldest brother appeared in front of me, his cry sharp and concerned.

I tried to tell him I was all right, but my knees buckled under the onslaught of pain. Harvey caught me before I fell, lifting me into his arms with unusual gentleness.

"Mother!" His call preceded his quick stride, and I tried to protest. He was moving toward the dining room, and I couldn't appear at my birthday meal covered in dirt and blood.

But Harvey ignored my mumbled words, bursting into the room in the most dramatic fashion possible. Cries and exclamations broke out, and a chair crashed to the ground.

"Really, this isn't necess—" I started to say, my words dying as I caught a glimpse of Faylee's concerned face.

Tears welled in my eyes at the knowledge that she would soon be looking at me differently. But the view of my guests was replaced with the face of my mother, shock rendering her silent for once. Her comforting presence released something inside me, and with all the fight gone, darkness swooped in to take its place.

CHAPTER 4

I woke in my own bed, feeling alert and well rested. But I jolted upright as soon as my memory returned, frantically feeling my injured arm. I could detect no sign of any injury, however.

I fell back against the pillows, gasping. Had I imagined the whole thing? I couldn't possibly have been sleeping long enough to heal completely.

"She's awake!" The bellow made me startle so badly I nearly toppled out of bed. I glared at my youngest brother, but he was turned toward the door shouting again for our mother.

"Are you trying to shatter my ear drums on top of everything?" I growled at Timothy, who at fourteen was all gangly long limbs and who usually preferred to communicate in grunts.

"When Harvey carried you into the dining room, you looked like you were dead," he said at a more normal volume, twisting back to me and grinning.

"Well, clearly I'm not," I said shortly, not wanting to think about the embarrassing moment.

"Even for you, it was a dramatic birthday meal." He leaned back in his chair. "And to think I thought it was going to be boring and tried to get out of attending."

I narrowed my eyes at him, but I couldn't muster any true antagonism. From the position of his chair by my bed, he had been watching over me, waiting for me to wake.

Then he continued speaking, extinguishing my goodwill.

"And now you're *finally* awake, so Mother will have to let me free. Did you have to sleep so long? I've been dying here."

I pushed myself into a sitting position, glaring at him. "*You've* been dying?"

He grinned. "Well, you just said you weren't."

My lips twitched, and his grin widened. Sandwiched in the middle of four brothers, I knew better than to take their sallies personally. For their part, they had decided years ago that I was a good sport and treated me accordingly, much to our mother's dismay.

Two tall figures appeared in the doorway at the same time, shouldering each other in their efforts to squeeze into the room first. I sighed at both of them but directed my words toward Anson.

"As the oldest, shouldn't you show a little more dignity?"

He scoffed. "Mother has been making us spend every spare minute that we're not at work kicking our heels at home. Anyone would think we were keeping vigil at your deathbed! I need to see with my own eyes that you're awake and I can finally be free."

Ellis, the brother between me and Timothy, snorted. "A tragedy, indeed! All the girls at the market must be despairing at the absence of their favorite flirt."

Anson smirked back. "Only the pretty ones."

I sighed loudly. "Are you trying to make me sick again?"

All three of them rushed quickly to my side, jostling each other as they plumped the pillows behind me and straightened my blankets.

"Dearest Aria," Ellis said. "Is there anything you need us to fetch? We are utterly dedicated to your full recovery."

"Yes, I can see that," I said dryly. "What was Mother thinking keeping you all chained here?" I held up my arm and moved it around experimentally, still unable to find any trace of the injury. "I'm completely fine. What in the kingdom happened?"

"Faylee," Anton said promptly. "Mother always said you'd done well coming to her notice, and she was proved right at last. Faylee had a healing composition on her, and she insisted on using it."

My brows rose. "Faylee was carrying a healing composition able to fix an injury like that?"

Timothy shrugged. "She said it was a side effect of that expedition into the mountains with the Sekali princess. The one that made her famous. She said she always keeps a stack of healing compositions on her."

"She has plenty of mage friends to supply them," Ellis added in an admiring tone. "And not just minor mages either—ones from the four great mage families."

"Our family is very grateful that she chose to use

compositions from her own personal supply on Aria," Anson said in a repressive tone.

Ellis glared at him resentfully but didn't say anything. I knew he hadn't meant to minimize Faylee's gift with his words. He had hero-worshiped her since the first time she visited my family.

Their mention of Faylee made me squirm uncomfortably, however. Had Zakary already visited her? She would be even more disappointed in me after giving me such a valuable gift. Even Zakary, a mage himself, hadn't had the necessary healing composition, and yet Faylee had gifted it to me without a thought.

I swung my legs around, determined to get up. If I remained stationary in bed, I would only feel worse and worse. If Faylee wanted to upbraid me, it was better to face it as soon as possible.

A head rush hit me as soon as I stood, however, and my vision briefly blurred. I put a hand out blindly to steady myself, and all three of my brothers lunged for me, keeping me upright.

"Quick, get a hold of yourself before Mother sees," Timothy hissed.

I rolled my eyes and pushed them all away. "I'm fine. I just got up too quickly. How long was I in bed for anyway?"

"Four horrifically long days," Anson said.

"FOUR DAYS!?" I nearly blacked out again. They had to be teasing me. "I cannot have been sleeping for four days."

"Faylee gave Mother two compositions," Timothy said. "The first was for healing, and the second was a working to encourage rest. Apparently, you have to rest after such a significant healing, and they seemed to think that would be a challenge where you were concerned."

He and Ellis exchanged smirks.

"Your body must have needed rest badly if the composition made you sleep for so long," Anson said more gently.

"How could you let me sleep for four days?!" I wailed, unable to process their words. "I've missed the last test."

"Exactly." My mother appeared in the doorway, regarding me with satisfaction. "Given how obsessed you were with that test, I knew I would never keep you in bed and resting without intervention. This was for the best."

"Mother, how could you?" My voice cracked and tears pricked at my eyes. "Byron is a Robart just like Gina, and now Teacher Wendell will have an excuse again, just like two years ago."

My mother's expression softened, and my brothers cleared their throats, exchanging looks that I caught in my peripheral vision. They weren't comfortable with my display of emotion, but they shared my anger over Teacher Wendell's previous betrayal.

Bustling over to me, my mother put a comforting arm around my shoulders. "It would be one thing if you had a chance. But everyone says the fourth-year trainees are strong this year. There isn't going to be a sealing ceremony this summer, and you would have put your health at risk for nothing."

I swallowed the lump in my throat, trying to blink back my tears. Mother had never understood the drive that pushed me to keep going after Gina stole my place.

"Big news!" The shouted words came from the front of the house. "Big news! Where are you all?"

"In Aria's room!" Anson called back, and my final brother appeared in the door, panting from an apparent run.

We all stared at him. At twenty, Harvey had mostly outgrown the youthful boisterousness that still plagued Ellis and Timothy. If he was this excited, it really was big news.

"They've caught the Shrouded Mage!" he gasped out, grinning at us all before his eyes fastened on me. "There's going to be a sealing ceremony after all!"

My mother gave a soft, astonished cry as I stumbled backward, sinking onto the bed. Their voices swirled around me, talking and exclaiming. Several supporting hands reached for me, but I pushed them all away.

After a few moments, my mother swept my brothers out of the room, pausing in the doorway herself.

"I'm so sorry, Aria," she murmured. "There's still a chance you'll be the one…"

I shook my head silently, not looking at her. I had missed the final test completely, not just performed below my usual standard. There was no way the teacher would miss his chance to choose another Robart. Everything I had worked for was over.

My family tiptoed around me over the following two days, not even pressing me to tell them how I had ended up injured on my birthday. They didn't mention my continued presence in the house either, no one asking why I was missing my final days of school.

But on the last day, I forced myself to leave the house at last. I had no hope that I would be chosen over Byron—my mother had informed the school of my injury while I was sleeping, but I knew that wouldn't weigh with Teacher Wendell—but I had to officially confirm the situation.

My appearance in the classroom proved just as awkward as I had anticipated. The happy hum and buzz of the end of the year dimmed the moment I appeared, and the admiring crowd around Byron stepped back slightly. Those who spoke to me did so in quiet, uncomfortable voices. Even the teacher fell back before my accusing eyes, addressing me in a brash, blustering tone that showed he had some shame lurking deep inside.

I left early. I didn't have any friends of my own left at school anyway. I had been the only eighteen-year-old left.

I couldn't bring myself to go straight home, though. As uncomfortable as school had been, my family weren't much better—tiptoeing around me as if I was still an invalid.

At least the visit to my school had provided the information that the sealing ceremony was to take place in two days' time. I would give myself those two days to wallow and grieve, I decided. And after the sealing ceremony was complete—sealing the hopes of my childhood and youth with it—I would think about the future and try to find a way to start fresh.

The thought seemed impossible. Despite my mother's attempts, I had defiantly refused to think about any other future path than being sealed and joining the University's commonborn class. At most, I had sometimes wondered if I might accept an offer of a job from Faylee after I was sealed, rather than attending the University. But given she was a Robart, I had never seriously considered it.

My steps led me aimlessly around the familiar streets that lay between my school and home. I knew this section of the lower city so well that I didn't need to pay attention to my path.

The thoughts that consumed me were unrelentingly dark. I had been overlooked for sealing again, rendering pointless every effort I had undertaken to ingratiate myself with my teacher. I had put myself in danger for nothing, and in the process I had given Zakary—the first mage I had ever properly met—a disgust of me. Even Faylee must have given up on me. Despite gifting me the compositions, she hadn't come to check on me since, so I could only assume Zakary had met with her and delivered the letter as promised.

"Aria!"

The unfamiliar voice calling my name made me start and look up. I didn't want to talk to anyone. If one of the locals—used to seeing me dashing back and forth between school and home—offered sympathy and commiseration, it would be unbearable.

But the young man who strode to my side wasn't a local. I stared at Zakary, trying to take in his presence. He was dressed as he had been at our first meeting—his appearance blending in with the commonborn population.

I wasn't at risk of mistaking him for a commonborn this time, however. His face had been burned on my memory after our short but intense interaction. And now that I was seeing him without the dishevelment of our first meeting, I could see subtle signs that he didn't fit. He carried himself with confidence despite his age, and his clothes, though understated, were well made and perfectly fitted to him.

"What are you doing here?" I blurted out, too shocked for niceties.

He glanced up and down the street before seizing my arm. Dragging me behind him, he hurried into a side alley, igniting memories of the attack.

I pulled my arm free and tried to peer over his shoulder. Surely he wasn't being pursued by fresh attackers?

When I looked back at him inquiringly, he was staring at me. I frowned, peering down at my dress.

"What's wrong?" I asked. "Is something amiss?"

He flushed and cleared his throat, looking away. "You just look different when you're not—"

"Covered in dirt and blood?" I grinned at him. "I was just thinking the same thing about you."

I snuck another look at my dress, remembering belatedly that I had dressed up for school, something I normally never did. But knowing the humiliation I would be walking into, I had needed the extra armor. It hadn't been enough, though, and I had forgotten my appearance in my wanderings around the city.

I snuck another glance at Zakary, my eyes lingering on his broad shoulders and the smooth fit of his shirt and leather vest. His arms looked as whole and undamaged as my own, so his healing must have been sufficient.

He cleared his throat again. "I was hoping I would run into you. I wanted to make sure you were all right." He nodded toward my arm. "You don't have a bandage, so you must have gone to a healing clinic after all. Do you need—?"

I cut him off, suddenly unable to bear him offering to cover the cost of the healing. At the beginning, I had fully intended to insist on it, but too much had happened to upend my life since then. Now it felt, however illogically, like it would be one humiliating blow too many.

"Yes, my arm is fine, as you can see."

"That's good, then." Zakary cleared his throat yet again, unaccountably awkward.

I let anger stir inside me, strong enough to wash away the humiliation. It had been this boy's fault that I had missed the final test and provided the teacher with the excuse he needed to choose Byron over me.

"I met with Faylee the day after the attack," Zakary continued when I said nothing.

"Of course you did." My words brimmed with resentment. "Since you hadn't sufficiently ruined my life already."

Zakary fell back a step, his eyes widening. "Ruined your life? I took a risk and didn't turn you in! I thought you *wanted* the letter delivered."

"What I wanted was to deliver the letter myself," I snapped. "What I wanted was to stay on my teacher's good side, to come first in the final test of the year, and to be chosen for sealing when the Shrouded Mage was caught. But then you had to get yourself attacked." I swallowed, forcing the flow of words to stop.

Zakary's brow creased. "What does my attack have to do with any of that? I delivered the letter and even intervened on your behalf with Faylee. Unlike me, she knows your teacher's identity, and she wanted to confront him.

But she promised not to do so when I pointed out that he would likely retaliate against you."

Shame washed over me. I was unloading my anger on Zakary when he had been trying to protect me.

He continued to watch me with concerned eyes. "I heard about the arrest. I thought…" He hesitated. "No one's going to fail the Academy this year, and you've just turned eighteen, so this sealing was a last-minute chance for you. I thought you'd be so excited."

My shoulders slumped. "My mother was worried I wouldn't rest after the healing."

"I can't imagine why," he murmured, but he said the words quietly, his eyes still showing concern.

"So she worked a second composition and forced me to sleep. For four days. I missed the final test."

"You slept for four days!?" His eyes widened. "From one composition? How much power did it have!?"

I shrugged uncomfortably. "My family thinks it must mean my body was in desperate need of rest."

Zakary nodded slowly. "Just how hard have you been driving yourself studying? You must have been on the point of collapse if your body shut down so completely in response to the rest composition."

"I only had to make it through one more week," I said, a little of my fire returning. "And then I could have slept for a week straight. I would have had all summer to prepare for the university year starting."

"You were planning to apply to the University?" A gleam of interest lit his eyes. But he must have realized I hadn't been chosen for sealing after all because the spark sputtered and died. "So your teacher chose someone else?"

I nodded. "Byron is a Robart. If I'd come first in that test, I could have lodged an official complaint over not being chosen. There would have been a review. But as it is…"

"And you only needed healing because you saved me." Zakary looked appalled, and my heart instantly contracted, my anger forgotten.

"It wasn't your fault you were attacked," I said quickly. "If anyone is to blame for this mess, it's those thieves who thought they'd try their hand at being copycat murderers." Fresh indignation filled me. "I just wish I'd recognized one of them. I would love to hand them over to the Reds."

Zakary's eyes slid away from mine, discomfort filling his face, although I couldn't imagine what had caused it.

"I need to go," he murmured, and my own face fell. I didn't try to stop him, though. How could I? I had no reason to keep him.

But as I watched him disappear down the street, his pace fast, my mood once again plummeted. At our first meeting, he had discovered me with illicit writing, and at our second, I had used him as the target for all the anger, frustration, and disappointment whirling inside me. Was it any wonder that he couldn't get away fast enough?

It wasn't until I was lying in bed that night that it occurred to me to wonder what he had been doing wandering around the lower city so soon after being attacked—and dressed, once again, like a commonborn. Was he asking to run into trouble?

Sighing, I rolled over and told myself that Zakary's mysteries had nothing to do with me. I wasn't likely to ever see him again.

CHAPTER 5

The next day I didn't leave my house. I told myself it was because I wanted to rest, but if I was honest, I didn't want to find myself scanning the streets for Zakary's absent face. Seeing him practically run from me had brought the reality of my future crashing in. I had hoped to win myself a position of value—to become someone like Faylee who was respected everywhere she went. But I would have to find a new, simpler dream now.

But while I could avoid the streets, I couldn't avoid my family. They all gathered for the evening meal except Anson, and the concerned looks my mother kept sending in my direction weren't as surreptitious as she thought.

"It's been too long since we did a day trip out of the city," Harvey announced suddenly. "I thought we could all go tomorrow."

"What?" Timothy protested. "But the Shrouded Mage is being sealed tomorrow! I heard they're going to march him through the streets to the sealing ceremony, and my friends are all planning to go watch."

"That's ridiculous!" Ellis exclaimed. "The Reds would never do that. What if he escaped?"

Timothy scoffed and began a hot reply, but Harvey cut him off with a significant look toward me.

"Oh. Yeah…" Timothy and Ellis exchanged uncomfortable looks and focused on their half-empty plates of food.

"I thought we could take a picnic down to the river," Harvey continued as if they hadn't interrupted.

I sighed loudly. "You can't all be tiptoeing around me forever. And I'm not going to spontaneously combust if I'm inside the city walls when the sealing ceremony takes place."

I managed a grin. "Although I do appreciate the thought, Harvey. Even if Mother was definitely the one to come up with the idea and pressure you into making the suggestion."

Ellis cackled. "Busted!"

"I'm so sorry, Aria." Tears clogged my mother's voice. "I never dreamed this would happen."

"I know. You were just worried about me." I stood and circled the table to give her an awkward side hug.

I had been furious with her in the first flush of my heartbreak, but my fury had burned out when I stood in front of Zakary and realized the true blame lay with the criminals.

And Teacher Wendell. I was reserving plenty of blame for him.

My mother hugged me back fiercely, and I barely extricated myself to return to my seat.

"You could come along with my friends to see the

Sealed Mage," Timothy offered tentatively. "Gordy decided last week that he's in love with you, so they won't mind."

I gaped at him. "Gordy thinks he's in love with me? But he's fourteen!"

Ellis shrugged. "All my friends think you're pretty." His expression and tone suggested this was a great mystery that he hadn't yet been able to fathom.

"They don't live with her," Timothy explained wisely. "And they haven't seen her when she's angry. That must explain it."

"I am not going to see the Sealed Mage with a fourteen-year-old who wants to make eyes at me," I said firmly.

"There's no point going at all," Ellis said in a superior tone. "The Reds aren't going to parade him through town."

"Gordy heard it from his sister whose husband works at—"

"I have to agree with Ellis on this one," I said, cutting off Timothy's spiel before it grew even more ridiculous. "They built the shielded hall for the sealing ceremonies at the main law enforcement hub, and that's sure to be the hub where they're keeping the Shrouded Mage. They have no need to parade him through the streets on the way to the ceremony."

"Exactly!" Ellis exclaimed. "They'll have been keeping him in the cells there from the start."

Timothy lapsed into sulky silence before suddenly shooting his closest brother a look. "And what will you be doing tomorrow instead, then?"

"Nothing that has anything to do with you," Ellis said too quickly, and Timothy gave him a disgusted look.

I glanced between them, interested despite myself. What did Timothy know that I didn't? Had Ellis found a new girl to chase?

"I can't approve of your strange fascination with such a violent person," my mother said, not seeming to notice the tension between her youngest sons. "I don't see why any of us need to lay eyes on him. In fact, I sincerely hope none of us ever do."

"As you've said every day since we first heard of his existence." I shook my head, but I was smiling.

"And what else would a mother hope for, I ask you?" she said with a return of her usual tart tone.

She stood to begin clearing the table, and we all clambered to our feet to help her. I tried to position myself so that I could manage a quiet question to Ellis, but he adroitly avoided me. And as soon as the table was cleared, he disappeared completely, although it was far too early for bed.

The next morning he didn't appear at the breakfast table at all, and curiosity got the better of me.

"Where's Ellis?" I asked Timothy. "What's he doing today?"

I didn't really expect him to answer—despite the squabbles, my younger two brothers had always been a pair, just as the older two were—but he muttered a single word under his breath. "Traitor."

I straightened, fixing him with my sternest older sister stare. "What does that mean? You tell me right now, Timothy! Or I'll...I'll find a snake to put in your bed."

Timothy threw me a horrified look. "See, if they saw

this side of you, none of our friends would think you were so pretty."

"Never mind that. You tell me what's going on with Ellis."

Timothy sighed and slumped as far into his chair as he could, as if he hoped to disappear beneath the table. "Ellis left the advanced school after only two years, but he's still friends with most of the boys his own age there."

I stared at him for half a second, not comprehending. Then everything became clear.

"Byron is the same age as Ellis!"

Timothy nodded, his eyes on his food. "All the sixteen-year-old boys are accompanying him to the sealing ceremony and waiting to see his wrists when he comes out."

"And Ellis is going with them?" I exclaimed, now understanding the label Timothy had given him. "Of all the traitorous…" I let my voice trail off with a wary glance at our mother who was coming toward the table with a fresh dish.

The kitchen door burst open, slamming against the wall as someone tumbled through the opening, gasping for breath. Mother dropped the dish she was holding, and it smashed, food spilling across the floor.

"Ellis!" she cried in indignation, glaring at the new arrival. "What in the kingdom are you—"

But he ignored her, his eyes on me as he struggled to speak through his panting breaths.

"Just…came…from the…law enforcement hub," he managed to pant out.

"Yes, I heard you went there," I said with narrowed eyes.

He waved a hand through the air as if to wave away such petty concerns.

"Heard...the clerk talking," he managed to get out.

Timothy straightened. "Don't tell me Byron's name wasn't on the list, after all? That would serve him right. I don't know why you're friends with such a poisonous toad. Last week, he said—"

"No. His name's there." Ellis's words became more comprehensible as he regained his breath. "But so is Aria's!"

"What?!" I leaped to my feet, my chair clattering to the floor behind me. "What do you mean? Are you sure?"

He nodded, gesturing frantically toward the doorway. "We were hanging around in the foyer of the law enforcement hub after Byron went in, and we heard two of the clerks talking. One was listing off the names of the people who hadn't arrived yet. And he said your name! I even asked to be sure, and it was definitely you."

"But I don't understand," I said, bewildered and frozen with shock. "What does that mean?"

"It means your name got on the list as well as Byron's," Ellis said. "It means your name is down to be sealed. *Today!*" he added when I didn't immediately move.

My mother sucked in an audible breath, looking between Ellis and me.

"Aria!" Timothy shouted, shoving me roughly in the back, propelling me toward the door.

"But...But how did it happen?" I asked, still struggling to make sense of Ellis's dramatic pronouncement.

"Never mind that," Timothy said. "The ceremony is

happening this morning, and who knows when the next one will be. You have to GO, Aria!"

His words finally penetrated the fog of my confusion. I strode toward the door, and Ellis stepped aside to let me through.

"Run!" he shouted after me as I stepped into the street, and I picked up my pace.

It made no sense. It was impossible. If I was on the list, I should have been informed, surely? And yet, administrative errors did occur.

I pushed the questions out of my mind so I could focus on running. It didn't matter how it had happened, as long as I made it there in time.

I dodged a wagon and leaped over a sack someone had dumped on the pavement while he chatted with a neighbor. The two men shouted after me, but I was already well past them.

I ducked and wove as I careened down the street, calling apologies over my shoulder whenever I bumped against someone. The ceremony being at the central hub meant it was closer to the palace and the sections of the city inhabited by the mage families than to my home.

My pace began to lag as my breathing grew labored. But the specter of missing the ceremony by seconds filled me with a second wind, and I increased my speed again.

I careened around a corner and onto South Road, the main street that ran all the way through Corrin to the palace itself. I had avoided it until the last possible moment, knowing it would be bustling with traffic. And sure enough, it was far busier than the smaller street I had just exited.

But ahead of me I caught a glimpse of free-standing red sandstone. I dodged three horses, a donkey, and an elaborate carriage, ignoring the shouts of disapproval that followed me down the street. Taking the steps into the building two at a time, I tripped, staggering into the foyer and nearly falling.

CHAPTER 6

"The sealing!" I cried loudly into the large space. "I'm here for the sealing."

"There's no need to shout about it." A disapproving clerk moved toward me.

I wanted to beg him to hurry, but I gasped for breath instead, hoping his stately pace meant I'd made it in time.

He carried a parchment in his hands, his sleeves pulled back to show the markings around his wrists. I looked at the paper greedily. Could it possibly be true that I would soon be able to read similar parchments, just as the law enforcement clerk could?

"Your name?" he asked, and I gave it.

"Yes," he grumbled. "It had to be. The last one."

Euphoria filled me. I really was on the list. Until that moment a strong shadow of doubt had lingered. Ellis would never play such a cruel prank on me, but he had been relying on secondhand information.

The clerk looked at me over the top of the parchment, his expression as disapproving as his voice. "You're cutting it mighty fine, young lady. We've never had someone not show up for their own sealing ceremony."

"I'm sorry," I gasped out. "I didn't know…" I let the words trail off, not clarifying what exactly I hadn't known. I didn't want to raise even the faintest suggestion that my name had somehow made it onto the list by mistake. "Where do I go?" I asked instead.

The clerk waved forward a young woman who wore the same red uniform of a law enforcement clerk but lacked any markings on her wrist. She led me through a side door and down a corridor.

"Usually people turn up early," she told me with a sideways glance. "I was starting to think I would have to slip in myself." She gave a soft laugh to show she was joking, but I felt a stab of pity for her anyway.

I had earned my place in the sealing ceremony, and I didn't feel bad for taking it. But the calculations on the number able to be sealed would have been precise. If I hadn't shown up, they certainly wouldn't have wasted a spot. There were probably already conversations underway as to who should be sent in at the last minute in my place.

Two guards and another clerk stood at the doorway of the actual hall, and I had to give my name again. The clerk crossed something off the list and nodded at one of the guards.

"That's the last one."

The second guard ushered me inside, and the door behind me was firmly closed, the click of a lock chasing me inside. I stood on trembling legs, looking around me.

I was no longer gasping loudly, but my breath still came

raggedly, my whole body shaking. It would take me more than a minute or two to recover from such a desperate and prolonged sprint. But I had made it, and that was all that mattered.

I had always imagined the ceremony to be a formal affair with rows of stiff seats and utter silence. Instead, I stood on the edge of a milling crowd. People stood tightly enough that there wouldn't have been room for everyone to be seated, and I could see no sign of any furniture at all.

The waiting throng stood in clusters, their murmurs creating a hum throughout the hall. But those closest to me turned to look at me with curiosity, and I managed a weak smile. I was still in too much shock to engage in proper conversation.

"They've finally locked the doors," one man said. "They should be bringing the mage in, in that case."

"Aren't you terrified?" A woman asked in a breathy voice. "To be in the same room as the Shrouded Mage?"

"Nonsense," the man said stoutly. "He'll be accompanied by plenty of guards, and he'll only have a single composition on him."

His words set off a fresh wave of murmurs from those around us. We all knew which composition the criminal would carry—the one that would connect to his energy and seal his power, along with the power of everyone within the shielded hall. For him, that would be a devastating blow, blocking his access to his power. But for those of us who couldn't control the power anyway, it would be a miraculous release. Once sealed, we would be able to write without unleashing uncontrolled power, and that meant we would be permitted to learn to read and to possess and handle written words.

"He must be a powerful mage," another woman said. "We're packed in here like sardines." She didn't sound upset about it, though. Maybe she would have been one of those to miss out on a place if there were fewer of us.

"Not powerful enough to be moved to the arena at the Mage Academy," a second man said. "I once met someone who was sealed at a ceremony there. There were too many of them to be squeezed into the hall that time."

"That's incredibly rare, though," the sardines woman said quickly. "I have a friend who was sealed five years ago. She said they had rows of seats for them, and even so, they only filled two thirds of the hall."

"I'm just glad to be here," the breathy woman said, and I nodded fervently.

A spreading wave of silence from the other side of the hall caught our attention, and we all craned to look. There must have been another door to the hall because four guards had entered, escorting a man who was shackled at the feet.

The man looked down at the ground, not making eye contact with anyone, and it was impossible to get a good look at him in the crowded room. The guards, looking almost as proud and excited as the other occupants of the room, led their prisoner into the center of the hall.

I caught a flash of one of their bare wrists and realized they had been assigned to guard duty because they had been chosen for sealing. No wonder they looked so pleased with their task.

I expected someone to say some official words—

perhaps to make a small speech. But I should have known better. There was no space for extraneous officials in this ceremony.

Instead, one of the guards prodded the bound man. "You know what you need to do," he said. "The doors are now locked, and the shield has been confirmed secure."

The man looked like he wanted to protest, but instead his shoulders slumped, and he ripped the piece of parchment in his hand in one swift movement, tearing it clean through. The sound carried through the now silent hall as every occupant held their breath.

I waited along with those around me, but nothing happened. I felt nothing at all.

One second passed and then another and another. I forced myself to breathe, glancing around at the others. Had anything even happened?

"Is...is it done?" a man closer to the guards asked in a carrying voice. "I don't feel any different."

One of the guards laughed. "I should think not. You'd have to be the Spoken Mage to sense something like that."

"Unless you sense something?" one of the other guards asked the prisoner curiously.

The man just shrugged, his head still slumped so low I couldn't see his face.

"No chance we'd sense anything," said the opinionated man near me, although he'd been looking unsure a moment before. "We can't sense power like the mageborn."

"Or energy like the Spoken Mage and those new energy mages," the sardine woman added.

"But then, how can we be sure it worked?" the breathy woman asked, sounding alarmed. "I don't want to find out something went wrong when I try to write and blow myself up."

The door behind me had been unlatched while she was speaking, but I didn't immediately turn to leave, too absorbed in her words. I felt a burning interest in the answer to her question.

A light laugh made me swing around, however. The young woman standing in the open doorway smiled warmly at the breathy woman.

"That exact fear is why I'm here. When you all file past to leave, I will ensure that everyone has, indeed, been sealed. I can feel it already in you."

The breathy woman's eyes widened, and she sank immediately into a deep curtsy. "Your Highness!"

The rest of the hall followed in her wake, a wave spreading outward as everyone bowed or curtsied, cries sounding on every side.

"Princess Elena!"

"The Spoken Mage!"

I sank into a wobbly curtsy, trying to copy the women around me without taking my eyes off the Spoken Mage. She was so close I could have reached out and touched her.

She met my eyes, amusement in hers. "I'm shorter than you imagined, aren't I?" she asked, and I nearly lost my balance completely.

"Not at all," I assured her fervently, meaning every word. "You're perfect."

Her eyes widened slightly, and she laughed. "I'm not sure any of my brothers would agree with you."

A laugh burst out of me, breaking past the awe that had rendered me witless and off balance.

"I have four brothers myself, Your Highness," I managed to say. "So I know what you mean."

"Four! Three is quite enough for me," she said with a chuckle.

Stepping back, she gestured for us to exit the hall, walking past her as we headed back toward the entrance to the building. The crowd surged forward, rushing past me and blocking my view of the princess who had once been a commonborn girl just like me.

I had been proud, thinking of Faylee as the most famous commonborn in Ardann. But that distinction actually belonged to Elena of Kingslee—even if she was now the most powerful mage to ever live, a Devoras, and a princess of Ardann.

And she had just spoken directly to me! My brothers were going to be so jealous.

I joined the stream of people filing through the door and received a warm smile from the Spoken Mage as I passed her.

"Hurry home and tell your brothers you're safely sealed," she murmured.

The line continued inexorably forward, sweeping me past her before I could reply, but her words echoed in my head. My sealing wasn't the only bit of news I would be sharing with my brothers. They wouldn't believe I had actually met and spoken to the Spoken Mage, the one who had changed everything for the commonborn of Ardann. The one who had given me my dream.

I didn't make it many steps further before I was greeted with a row of guards. They weren't facing toward me, though, but away, back toward the foyer, as if guarding against anyone else joining us. With our passage forward blocked by their presence, our line snaked sideways, passing through another door into a smaller room.

I expected to find people bunched up before me, but the room held another door on the opposite wall, allowing the flow of movement to pass smoothly through one door and out another. Inside the room, we were ushered into two lines, filing past two desks that each held a large stack of parchments. A clerk sat behind each desk, and as a person approached them, they ripped one of the parchments, flicking their fingers toward the person.

I craned my head to the side, staring with fascination at the people ahead of me. Within seconds of a composition being worked, the skin pigment around the indicated person's wrists changed. I took a step sideways to get a better view, but a guard frowned at me, and I shuffled back into line.

"Keep moving!" another guard called, clearly trying to keep the line moving as efficiently as possible.

They had their job cut out for them since everyone who had passed the desks moved slowly, their eyes glued to their wrists. I determined I would keep up my pace, regardless, but when the clerk's fingers flicked in my direction, I nearly stumbled over my own feet, despite my intentions.

Unlike the power from the pain relief composition which Zakary had flicked toward me, there was no physical sensation to accompany the working this time. But I could see its result, and as I shuffled forward, I couldn't tear my eyes away from the intricate pattern of darker skin pigment that would mark me forever as a sealed commonborn.

Once we exited the room on the far side, we were set free to mill into the foyer and spill out into the street. Crowds of people waited, either in the foyer or just outside the building—friends and family gathered to congratulate those newly sealed.

I caught sight of Teacher Wendell standing with a small clump of people who I was fairly certain were Robarts, reminding me that Byron must have been in the crowd with me somewhere. I hadn't caught sight of him, and I didn't make any effort to do so now, ducking sideways to stay out of my old teacher's line of vision.

Whatever had happened to get my name on the list for the sealing ceremony, I was certain it wasn't through the efforts of my teacher. He didn't have that kind of influence.

As I descended the steps of the law enforcement building, the answer hit me, blindingly obvious. It must have been Faylee. She was the only person I knew with enough power to get a name added to the list, and she had always felt guilty for what had happened with Gina. She must have felt even worse when she heard another cousin of hers had been chosen over me. She might still be angry at what I'd done, but she was a fair dealer.

I floated down the steps in a daze. I would have to find some way to thank her. She'd only just left on a trade expedition to the Sekali Empire that would take the whole summer at least, but that would just give me time to think of an appropriate gesture of gratitude. It didn't matter how long it was until I saw her again. Just like the marks on my wrists, my gratitude would never fade.

I wove through the crowds on South Road at a much more reasonable pace than my headlong flight to the ceremony. I didn't notice any details of the people around me, though, my shock muting my surroundings.

Thankfully, my feet knew the path home, and I made it off South Road and into the quieter back streets. Turning onto the largest of the roads in my district, I vaguely noted someone tall in my path. Stepping to the side, I tried to skirt around them, but the figure stepped sideways at the same moment I did, and I collided with a firm chest.

Bouncing back, I gasped and looked up into a familiar face. Zakary.

He grinned down at me, catching me around my forearms to steady me while I stared up at him. His appearance was yet another shock in a day that had been full of them. While I couldn't have failed to recognize him, he looked completely different from the times I'd seen him previously.

"You're wearing a white robe," I said blankly. "You're a trainee at the Academy."

"And you're sealed." His hands ran lightly down to my wrists, lingering for the briefest second on the marked skin there. A shiver ran up my arms.

"But if you're a trainee, how come you weren't wearing your white robe before?" I asked, my mind determinedly stuck on this small detail.

"We aren't required by law to wear them at all times." He chuckled. "And they're rather conspicuous."

"You didn't mention you were a trainee either," I said stubbornly, and he shook his head.

"Has being sealed made you more suspicious?" He

grinned. "My status as a trainee isn't a conspiracy, I promise. But if it makes you feel better, I'll only be a trainee for a few more days."

I stared at him. So he was a fourth year, about to graduate the Mage Academy. That meant I had been right in my first assessment that he was a couple of years older than me.

He chuckled again. "You seem excessively shocked. Are mage trainees so very shocking?"

I shook my head, holding up my wrists. "I was sealed today."

A grin pulled at his mouth. "I noticed. Congratulations."

"But I didn't know about it." The words tumbled over each other now that I'd started. "I had no idea and was just sitting at home eating my breakfast! Can you imagine? I nearly missed my own ceremony."

"What?" His brows drew together, but I barely heard him, the flow of words continuing.

"I was just sitting there when my brother burst in to say my name was on the list. They all started shouting to run, and I sprinted through half the city to get there in time." I barely paused for breath. "Well, it felt like half the city. I've never run so fast in my life! I was almost dying by the time I got there, but I made it. And then they brought the Shrouded Mage in. But I couldn't see his face. And I couldn't feel anything when he sealed me, but then the Spoken Mage appeared."

I grabbed his arm, my eyes shining up at him. "She spoke to me, Zakary! The Spoken Mage spoke to *me*! And she checked I was really sealed, and I really, truly am. And she has lots of brothers too! I didn't know that."

Zakary chuckled. "That does all sound very shocking." A shadow crossed over his face. "I'm just glad you made it."

I gave a shuddering sigh. "Me too. Can you imagine?" I shook my head, distracted for a moment at the awfulness of the possibility. "Faylee must have gotten my name included, but she's just left for a trip to the Sekali Empire. She must have assumed the officials would contact me, and they must have assumed she'd tell me herself."

"Faylee," Zakary said slowly. "Yes, I suppose I can see how a mix-up like that might happen if someone got involved who wasn't normally part of the process."

"But never mind," I said, too elated to dwell on anything negative. "It doesn't matter because it all worked out."

He smiled down at me, the warmth in his eyes suggesting my overwhelming joy was infectious. "Thank goodness for that." His lips twitched again, and he leaned forward, reaching for my hair.

For a moment, my breath caught in my throat, all thoughts of the sealing ceremony driven impossibly from my mind. Then he pulled back, a small piece of scrambled egg in his hand.

"I think you ran out of your house in such a rush that some of your breakfast went with you."

"What?!" I screeched, my hands flying to my hair as the awareness of my disheveled appearance crashed over me.

"Don't worry," Zakary said quickly, his lips still twitching. "You still look enchanting, I swear."

"You don't understand!" I wailed. "The Spoken Mage just saw me with breakfast in my hair!"

He swallowed the laugh that clearly wanted to come.

"Never mind," he said. "She must meet hundreds of people. She probably won't even remember you."

I glared at him. "Is that supposed to be reassurance? Because if so, you're terrible at it."

He laughed. "My apologies." He glanced up the road, his expression regretful. "I'd walk you home, but I have to get back to the Academy. My days there aren't quite over, and my combat instructor doesn't believe in tardiness."

I gasped. "You have classes today? What are you doing standing around here then? Quick, Zakary! Hurry!"

He threw one last look at me, half-full of laughter, half regret, and then began jogging away, back toward South Road. He stopped after a few steps, though, looking back over his shoulder.

"You should call me Zak. All my friends do."

Before I could think of a reply, he was jogging again. I watched him go in bemusement. What had he meant by that? Were we *friends* now?

And what had he been doing in the lower city on a class day?

A thought crept through my mind. Was it possible he had come especially to see me? Had he heard I was being sealed, even though I hadn't heard myself? He could read, so he might have seen the list.

I turned back toward home, floating rather than walking after the unexpected encounter. Zakary wouldn't have told me to call him Zak unless he thought we would see each other again. Maybe being sealed really did make a difference.

CHAPTER 7

*E*llis was feted by my family almost as much as I was that evening, and not even Timothy mentioned a word about treachery. If Ellis hadn't gone to wait outside the ceremony, our family would have missed our chance.

I was floating so high in the air I could even forgive Gina and Byron. I might forget that the next time I saw Byron strutting down the street, but for one night at least, everyone who passed through my mind was covered in a reflected glow.

I told the story of my conversation with the Spoken Mage over and over again at the demand of my brothers and parents, and my brothers pestered me for any detail of the Shrouded Mage's appearance as well. But I didn't mention meeting Zakary to anyone. I still hadn't told my family what had happened on my birthday, and none of them knew I had met a mage.

Not just met. I whispered to myself. *Befriended.*

They probably wouldn't believe it if I told them, and I

wasn't yet confident to share my secret with anyone. Part of me still expected Zakary to forget about me once he graduated. He would be starting his adult life and would have little reason to think about a commonborn girl he had met a handful of times.

If I was smart, I would do the same and put him out of my mind. But it wasn't so easy to do. For as long as I could remember, I had driven myself forward in pursuit of one goal. Even during summer breaks, I never let my studies slip.

And now I had finally achieved that goal. The constant focus of my life had gone, and my mind seemed determined to put Zakary into the empty space. But while I had made it over the finish line, I couldn't allow myself to collapse. Because it wasn't actually a finish line but a starting post.

In the autumn I would start at the University—my sealing had guaranteed me a place in their commonborn class. I had no idea how difficult the classes would be, but I did know that if I wanted to keep up, I needed to learn to read and write before I started. Sealing had given me the ability to write safely, but it hadn't instantly granted me the knowledge of words. I would have to do the work to acquire that myself.

I knew what that meant, but I procrastinated doing it. I didn't normally let myself procrastinate—I couldn't afford the time. But on this occasion, I couldn't seem to force myself to take the action I needed to take.

"Any news from any of your friends, Ellis?" My mother asked one evening over the dining table.

Her odd question would have made me curious except

for the obvious look she directed at Ellis, inclining her head in my direction. I sighed and took another mouthful. There was no point trying to stop whatever was coming. There never was where Mother was concerned.

"Oh yes," Ellis said stiffly, overacting his nonchalance so badly that Timothy rolled his eyes. "Byron started his reading lessons with Teacher Wendell yesterday."

"How wonderful!" my mother exclaimed, managing a slightly more normal air than my brother. "How fortunate he is. What a wonder it would be to be able to read!"

I winced as her words hit home. Staying near home for the last few days had meant I hadn't even had the opportunity to peek at words. To do that, I needed to go somewhere where books and writing were allowed. Somewhere like my school, where our sealed teacher kept his writing under careful lock and key, bringing it out only to read aloud to the class—and during those summers when one of his pupils had been sealed and needed to learn to read and write.

I didn't take my mother's bait, however, merely munching on in silence. She stared at me, and I counted down in my head. She had been unnaturally forbearing for days. There was no way she was going to be able to hold it in.

I only made it to four, so she was obviously more worried than I'd realized.

"Don't you want to learn to read, Aria!?" she exclaimed, throwing her hands in the air. "I thought it was your life dream. You used to go on about it often enough."

"Of course I want to read." I scooped up another spoonful. "But I've got all summer. There's no rush."

"No rush!?" Timothy shook his head. "If I'm ever sealed, I'll be looking for books immediately. Aren't you curious?"

"Of course I'm curious." Heat crept into my voice, despite my resolution not to be baited. "But I'm also tired. There's nothing wrong with taking a small break after all my hard work."

The irritation in my voice wasn't really for Timothy. He was right. And I'd always thought I'd immediately seek out words as well. Even in that moment, sitting at my family dining table, I felt a pull toward them.

But it wasn't the words I was avoiding. It wasn't even the work I would have to put in to understand them. I was avoiding the person who held the key to unlocking the longed-for knowledge.

My mother's face softened. "Of course you deserve a break, Aria dear. You've worked incredibly hard. I'm just concerned…"

She cast an anxious look toward my father, and he cleared his throat. "I've never liked the way that teacher of yours bows and scrapes to the Robarts," he said in his slow, deep voice. "Even before the incident two years ago."

Rumbles of anger sounded around the table from my brothers, dying down only at a glare from our mother. I kept my focus on my father, though. He was usually slow to pass judgment on others or to express an opinion on anything outside his field of expertise. I had known he was upset for me, but I'd never heard him criticize Teacher Wendell outright.

"It's for exactly that reason that your mother and I are concerned," he said. "If you miss your chance to join the

Robart boy in learning to read, there's every chance your teacher will refuse to teach you at all."

I frowned. That possibility hadn't occurred to me.

"Could he do that?" Anson sounded skeptical. "I thought teachers were required to run a summer reading class if anyone from their class was sealed during the last year."

"Indeed," my father rumbled. "And Teacher Wendell is running such a class. But if Aria misses the crucial early teaching, he may well claim that it's too late for her to join and that he isn't obligated to teach a second class."

I put down my spoon, my stomach suddenly churning too much for me to eat another bite. Why hadn't I thought of that? It sounded exactly like something that snake would do.

I steeled myself. "I'll go tomorrow," I managed to say, although it did little to settle the roiling in my stomach.

My mother, however, was instantly transformed. Wreathed in smiles, she bustled off to bring out an elaborate dessert that I couldn't bring myself to touch.

My family already didn't like my teacher, but they didn't know all of it. They didn't know the danger he had put me in with his laziness, or the way he had so easily turned his back on me after exploiting my desperation. It sickened me to think of spending long days in his company again.

But the next morning I forced myself to rise and dress promptly, leaving my house with dragging steps. I exited through the kitchen door, rounding the corner of the house to find a person on our front step, hand raised to knock.

"Zakary!" I rushed forward and grabbed his arm to stop him from knocking. "What are you doing here?"

"Visiting you, of course." He smiled at me. "And I'm relieved to see I'm at the right house. I was having last minute doubts about my information."

"How did you find out where I live?" I hissed as I dragged him away from the house, looking furtively from side to side as I did.

If a single person from our neighborhood saw us, they would find an excuse to go nosing to my mother with questions within the hour. And my mother currently knew nothing about the existence of any *tall, handsome stranger keeping Aria company.*

I dragged him down a side alley, skirting several dubious piles of detritus with a wrinkled nose. But as soon as I was confident we were out of sight, I whirled on him.

"Well?" I demanded. "How did you find me?"

He looked at me with bemusement. "There aren't a lot of Arias who just got sealed in this neighborhood."

"You've been asking people about me?" I cried in a despairing wail. "Zakary!" It would be less than an hour before someone turned up on my mother's doorstep.

"It's Zak, remember." But his face looked guilty now. "Should I not have asked about you? I wanted to talk to you, and I didn't know how else to find you now that you're finished with that school."

"If only," I muttered.

"But all the commonborn schools have started their summer break. Even the Academy has had their graduation now." He frowned. "And don't you finish at the local school once you're sealed regardless?"

The crease between his brows and the confused, concerned look in his eyes made me want to reach out and touch his face. I sternly suppressed the instinct, reminding myself I was supposed to be annoyed. I couldn't continue to muster the emotion, however, so I sighed.

"Never mind, what's done is done, I suppose. At least I know to brace myself for my mother's questions."

Zak's brow cleared, and he laughed. "I didn't think of that. But I can imagine. There would be plenty of people at my home asking questions if our roles were reversed."

I stiffened at his mention of his family. Whereas my mother would be painfully delighted I had befriended a mage, his mother was likely to have very different feelings about the situation.

He looked at me with renewed concern. "But why do you still need to go to the school? I thought you would be out from under that man's influence now."

I groaned. "I only wish I was. I never want to see him again. And the last student I want to spend the summer with is Byron. But I don't know anyone other than Teacher Wendell who can teach me to read and write, so I'm stuck with them both a while longer."

Zak's face immediately lightened. "If that's all it is, there's no problem at all."

I gave him a baleful look. "That's easy for you to say."

He grinned at me. "I think you're forgetting you do know someone else who can read and write."

I stared at him blankly. "Faylee's gone off on an expedition to the Sekali Empire and won't be back until at least the end of the summer, remember."

"I wasn't talking about Faylee, silly." He looked at me

with a smug expression as if waiting for me to see the obvious. When I continued to stare at him blankly, he gestured at himself. "I do know how to read and write, you know. I could hardly have just graduated the Academy if I couldn't."

"You!" I blinked. "Well, obviously you know how to read, but you're hardly going to teach me."

"Why not?"

I stared at him, unable to think of anything to say.

"Do you really think I'd be such a terrible teacher?" he asked, pretending hurt.

"Do you have any idea how long it's going to take?" I shook my head. "I'm not going to be reading fluently in a couple of hours."

His face turned serious, although his eyes shone with something I couldn't read. "Of course not. I expect it will take you all summer—and you'll have to work at it intensively. But clearly you have a lot of experience at working intensively."

"Why would you want to spend your entire summer teaching me to read?" I asked incredulously.

He cleared his throat. "Actually, I'm hoping for a favor in return."

He fixed me with pleading eyes, but I narrowed my own in response. The future I had worked so hard for was finally before me, and I wasn't risking it with any more foolish or illegal favors.

"The truth is that, unlike you, I'm a terrible student," he said in a rush.

"I—wait, what?" Whatever I had imagined him saying, it

hadn't been that. I frowned suspiciously. "Didn't you just graduate?"

"Yes, but the Academy is different. Half our training is in combat, and the other half is in compositions and controlling our power. I find those interesting, naturally, so that was easy."

"Then what's the problem?" I asked, still not understanding. "Aren't you supposed to be joining a mage discipline now? Won't it just be more compositions and the like?"

He sighed. "That was my plan. But my parents are utterly determined for me to go to the University."

I raised my brows. "You're terrible at study, but they want you to spend years at the University and—what? Become an academic or an official? That sounds like a terrible idea."

"Exactly!" he cried. "And so I've told them a hundred times. But they both studied at the University themselves and are now academics. They're convinced I need to keep my options open and that this is the best way."

I shook my head at the foolishness of that. I had seen plenty of youth come through the advanced class who were only there because their parents pushed them to keep studying, despite their lack of inclination or ability. They never lasted.

But Zak wasn't a dependent child, forced to follow his parents' wishes. Unless he was still dependent on them financially. Some minor mage families were significantly poorer than a merchant family like the Robarts. They wouldn't tutor or sell their compositions otherwise.

"If you join a discipline, don't you receive a salary?" I

asked. "You might have to live modestly at first, but I'm sure you could make it work." I had no idea how much graduated mages were paid when they first entered a discipline, but surely it was enough to live on. "If you need help finding affordable accommodation, I'm sure I could point you in the right direction."

He chuckled to himself, not seeming offended by my suggestion but clearly amused at something I didn't understand. "I can just imagine my parents' response to that."

He shook his head. "No, I'm not willing to risk their ire." He shrugged, not quite meeting my eyes. "You probably think me very cowardly, but I foresee that I'm going to need all the parental goodwill I can muster at some point in the future, and I don't want to burn that goodwill now. I have, therefore, agreed to at least start at the University. They've agreed that we'll reassess after the first year. If it's a disaster, then I'll apply to another discipline next summer."

I supposed one year wasn't much of a loss, although I didn't know if it would hurt his chances of being accepted by his chosen discipline. Then my mind caught up with the most important aspect of the situation.

"But that means we'll be starting at the University together!" I immediately flushed and added, "Although I'll be in the commonborn stream, of course, and you'll be in the mage classes."

"Exactly!" he sounded triumphant. "And unlike me, you're not a terrible student. You're an excellent one. So I'm willing to spend the summer teaching you how to read and write if you'll tutor me in return."

My mouth fell open. "You want *me* to tutor *you*?"

"Why not?" He grinned. "You are sealed now, remember?"

I looked slowly down at the pattern around my wrists, a smile growing on my face. "I suppose I am."

"So you'll do it?" He sounded eager, although I couldn't imagine why he found the prospect of intense study all summer so appealing.

I knew why I found the idea appealing, though. I snuck a glance at him, sucking on the inside of my cheek.

Zak was dangerous. There was no other way of putting it. He was attractive in ways that only seemed to grow every time I saw him. If it was hard enough to put him out of my mind now, how hard would it be after spending every day with him all summer?

The thought of being stuck in a classroom with Byron and Teacher Wendell every day of the summer flashed into my mind. My hand moved of its own accord, reaching out to shake Zak's.

"Deal," I said with more confidence than I felt as his warm, strong fingers gripped mine.

I would just have to guard my heart very, *very* closely. And hope that exposure lessened the effect he seemed to have on me.

CHAPTER 8

I had to tell my family about the arrangement. There was no avoiding that. But thankfully none of them had yet gotten a glimpse of Zak, so I was able to present the whole thing as a simple business arrangement.

My mother was predictably overjoyed, saying that it would be worth something indeed for me to start at the University already having a mage acquaintance. My father only said that he was glad I had found a way to avoid the Robart puppet.

I smiled and agreed with everything both of them said, not wanting to encourage them to ask more questions. If Zak and I were really going to study together all summer, one of my family members was bound to spot him eventually, and then the questions and suspicions would come. It was inevitable when Zak looked…the way he looked. But I was hoping to put that day off as long as possible.

My first concern had been where we would study—we needed access to books as well as parchment and pens, and we wouldn't find those in many places in the lower city. Certainly nowhere where they weren't secured.

But Zak had been ready with an answer, one I should have thought of for myself. Nearly five years ago, after the sealing ceremonies began in earnest, the crown opened an office for the management of sealed affairs. It was built on the outskirts of the city, near the outer wall, and had occasioned great excitement at the time. All four of my brothers had found excuses to visit the area when the creator mages were razing the derelict building that had stood there previously and raising a new, sturdy public building of red sandstone in its place. Even I had detoured past the building on occasion, thinking proudly of the day when my name would be on the lists kept within its walls.

"I already investigated," Zak told me. "They have a small library that's open for use by any sealed commonborns. And they have a whole series of study rooms. You can even request a locker where you'll be able to keep your parchment and pens stored between sessions, since you can't take them home. In the long term, you'll want to set up a safe place in your house to secure them. The office for the management of sealed affairs are also the ones to review and approve those arrangements. But you might not be able to do that until after you graduate the University and get a home of your own. And so we can use the lockers in the meantime."

When we actually stepped into the building for the first time, I buzzed with excitement, my arms bare and wrists on clear display. It still felt surreal that I had the right to freely enter a building that contained a library.

When an official bustled over to us, a frown on her face,

I held out my hands hurriedly, words ready on my lips. But they died when I saw that her attention was fully focused on Zak, not me.

"We don't take applications for being sealed here," she said firmly. "You'll need to apply through one of the usual channels. And in the meantime, I can't permit you entry since we have—"

I laughed, unable to help myself. Zak had returned to his old way of dressing, and I had thought from the beginning that his choice of clothes made him blend in. If he was wearing a mage robe, he wouldn't confuse anyone, but presumably he wouldn't have the right to wear a black University robe until he actually started there in the autumn.

The official turned her disapproving expression on me, and I tried to cut off my giggles. "He's my tutor," I said since it was close to the truth and by far the simplest explanation. "My *mage* tutor. He doesn't have any need to be sealed."

Her face immediately cleared. "That explains it. My apologies, My Lord."

Her attitude was brisk rather than obsequious, but I still felt a shiver of discomfort at her use of the general honorific for mages. I had never once used it, given the unusual circumstances of our acquaintance, but I couldn't afford to forget who Zak really was.

"I know the faces of all the usual tutors," the woman continued. "But I don't recognize you."

"That's because I only just graduated the Academy," he said with an easy smile.

"Ah, I see." She smiled a little more readily. "Do you need a tour of our facilities?"

Zak easily took charge, charming the woman even as he commandeered her to show us around. I watched him uneasily, reminded that he might only be two years older than me, but he had been born and bred for the kind of command I would never wield. It came all too naturally to him.

He organized a locker for our use, along with slate and chalk for me and a pile of parchment for him. But when we finally stood on the threshold of the library, my legs shook so badly, I struggled to take the necessary step that would carry me inside. After a lifetime of resisting the allure of books and words—of carefully avoiding them, no matter how much my curiosity burned—it seemed impossible that I was being allowed, even encouraged, to step into a room that contained whole shelves of books.

The official, who had largely forgotten me in the face of Zak's charm offensive, looked back, her expression softening. "You were sealed in the recent ceremony?" she asked gently.

I nodded, my mouth too dry for speech.

"It will become normal soon, if you can believe it. It's why I like showing the newcomers around. It's good to remember what it felt like the first time."

"Come on, Aria," Zak said with a grin. "You won't learn to read standing out there."

I took a deep breath and stepped over the threshold.

～

We met at the office of sealed affairs most days after that. My initial awe was soon replaced with frustration as I developed a hatred for my slate. I might have been surrounded by books, but I was clearly a long way from being able to read any of them.

Thankfully, I knew how to work hard, and slowly I made progress. Zak wasn't equally dedicated to his own studies, but he showed endless patience with me and seemed to find satisfaction from my progress. Privately, I thought he made a better teacher than a student. If he failed to gain admittance to a discipline after his year at the University, I would suggest he consider tutoring. It might not be prestigious, but it was possible to earn good coin from families like the Robarts.

I usually brought myself food from home to last me for the day, but at least once a week, Zak lured me out to a local food stall, or even to one of the markets to buy something hot and fresh. He always dressed in the same manner, making it easy for the two of us to blend in with the crowds of commonborn in the lower city, and usually he seemed relaxed and natural, despite the setting.

When we walked, we talked of things beyond our studies—our families, our plans for the future, foolish pranks of our childhood, and anything that occurred to us.

But every now and then, he would insist we take a sudden detour, usually through a less frequented alley or street, and he didn't like taking the same route too often. I refrained from questioning his odd behavior because I could easily guess the reason for it. Even mages sometimes had reasons to visit the lower city, and they certainly had servants. It made sense that Zak would sometimes spot someone he knew.

His desire to keep our association secret wasn't flattering, but I couldn't be surprised that he didn't want to be seen with me by anyone he knew. He might be a tutor for the summer, but he still had hopes of joining a discipline and rising above the rank of mages who were reduced to such activities.

It helped that his odd, erratic behavior suited my purposes as well. His desire for novelty meant we rarely visited markets near my home, and even when we walked together, it was down less frequented routes. As far as I knew, no one in my family had yet laid eyes on Zak.

Some days I put aside my own progress to insist we focus on Zak's studies, and he gradually grew more interested. During our time walking the city, I had learned that his two favorite disciplines were the growers and the creators, since they were both focused around creation, although in different ways. Zak had a fascination with how systems worked and seemed to have a natural instinct for how they could be improved. Wanting to prove myself an equally good teacher, I directed his studies toward topics that would interest him, igniting his curiosity.

"I'll admit that studying with you is more engaging than I expected," he told me. "And I liked the practical studies at the Academy, too. But at the University, the studies are much more academic. Even if I focus on one of my preferred disciplines, I'll have to write endless essays on the discipline's history, as well as cataloging the full breadth of Ardann's knowledge on all relevant topics."

"What's wrong with that?" I asked, and he laughed.

"You really are a true student, Aria. Unlike me, you're going to love the University."

"I hope so." I fell silent for a minute imagining it.

I hadn't visited the impressive University building yet, not even stepping inside its grounds. I didn't dare walk through the gates until I was officially a student. But I was glad to have spent so many weeks growing accustomed to the sealed affairs' office and its library. I was much less likely to embarrass myself when I first arrived at the University now.

"I think you might be rubbing off on me, though," he said. "When I see your joy at learning, I feel a sort of faint itch. Possibly a small twinge."

I glared at him suspiciously. "You make it sound like you're ill."

"I think I might be," he said gravely. "I feel the faintest echoes of..." He dropped his voice to a whisper. "Enjoyment at learning."

I whacked him lightly on the arm as I laughed, glad we were alone in our study room. If any other students were in earshot, they would be giving us disapproving looks for disturbing their peace.

"You're ridiculous," I said. "I don't know how you'll last a month at the University."

"Neither do I," he said with exaggerated sadness. "Maybe, as my official tutor, you could drop a word in my parents' ears?"

My amusement instantly dropped away. His parents didn't want to hear anything I had to say, especially where their son was concerned.

Zak's eyes also clouded for a brief moment, but he

quickly turned the subject and soon had me laughing again. Somehow he always managed to do that, no matter how tired I was or how frustrated at my progress. And in all the hours we studied together, he also got lost sometimes in our camaraderie and forgot who I really was.

The first time I managed to read a whole sentence without faltering, I jumped to my feet in triumph. Zak whooped, leaping to his feet as well and seizing me. He swung me around in a wide circle, knocking over at least two chairs.

I grinned at him, giddy with triumph, until awareness of our position crashed over me. His hold was little different from an embrace. As soon as my face froze, realization hit him as well, and he must have remembered I wasn't one of his Academy friends. He dropped me, stepping back and clearing his throat awkwardly.

"It's a start," I said quickly, trying to be the one to cover over the awkwardness for once. Had he noticed the flush in my cheeks? "But I'm going to need to read much more complicated words at the University."

"Sadly, that's true." He stooped to pick up the fallen chairs, hiding his face in the process. "But I have full confidence in you. Given the pace you've been learning so far, I'm convinced there's nothing you couldn't achieve if you put your mind to it."

I smiled, but my heart wasn't in it. It didn't matter how hard I tried or how much I achieved, I could never make myself into a mage. Only bloodlines could do that. And without the ability to control power, I could never be more than tutor and student—or at a stretch, friend—with a mage.

But times are changing, whispered an insidious voice in my mind. *The Spoken Mage has changed everything.*

I tried to ignore the alluring words, but sometimes when I lay awake in the darkness, I couldn't help turning them over in my mind. The gap between the sealed among the commonborns and the minor mages was closing. Everyone said so, even if they said it in whispers.

The changes had little effect on the great families—the powerful members of Devoras, Stantorn, Callinos, and even the Ellingtons—but it was different for the minor mage families. You only had to look at the power of commonborn families like the Robarts—and they'd never had a mage among them.

Maybe...just maybe, I wasn't imagining the warmth in Zak's eyes when they rested on me. Maybe he didn't look at me and see nothing but a commonborn.

But the minor mage families weren't happy about the changes happening in Ardann. They had the most to lose in this new social order, and Zak had already shown that he wouldn't go against his parents' wishes on matters of significance.

So, at the end of the day, it didn't matter how Zak saw me. There was still an insuperable barrier between us.

CHAPTER 9

$\mathcal{I}$ had grown so used to Zak and my routine that I had forgotten the danger of discovery by my family. So it took me entirely by surprise when I stepped out of the kitchen one morning and found my second oldest brother leaning against the wall of the alley beside our house, arms crossed. I took one look at his face and knew he was waiting for me and he wasn't happy. But for one blank moment, I couldn't think why.

"I saw you in the market yesterday," he said, not relaxing his posture. "With your *tutor*."

My cheeks instantly betrayed me with a flush, and his face tightened. "Yes, exactly."

"I don't know what you mean," I said, rallying. "Zakary *is* my tutor."

"That may be," Anson said. "But he also attracted the attention of every woman below thirty who caught sight of him."

I managed a laugh. "Now I see why you're looking so sour. Did he distract your latest flirt?"

He straightened, his arms dropping, but he looked sad rather than annoyed. "I saw the way you looked at him, too."

My flush deepened, but I managed to speak with dignity. "We've been working together for weeks and weeks now. Of course we've become friends. It's just what Mother was hoping for."

"Mother is not hoping that you get your heart broken," he said. "Because you know that's what's going to happen, Aria. He's a *mage*."

My chest tightened, but I couldn't bring myself to dispute any part of what he'd said. I clenched my teeth together, my shoulders slumping.

"I know," I said softly. "And it's true that I have eyes, the same as all those other girls. But that's all it is, I swear. I'm well aware that Zakary and I will only ever be friends."

"And maybe not even that once you're both at the University." Anson's words held a heavy warning. "It's one thing for him to slum it with you in the lower city during the summer. But he'll sing a different tune when he's only yards from the palace with his mage friends around him."

I wanted to protest that Zak wasn't like that. Obviously we'd see less of each other once the university year started, but he wouldn't completely abandon me either. I couldn't be entirely sure of that, though. Not when he kept ducking off our path at odd moments. And even if I was sure, the claim wouldn't do anything to reassure Anson.

"You haven't said anything to Mother, have you?" I asked sharply, a fresh worry hitting me.

"Do I need to?" His eyes rested heavily on my face.

"No," I said quickly. "You know what she'll be like." I gave him a pleading look.

He sighed. "Ellis and Timothy's friends aren't the only ones to have noticed you, Aria." He caught my look of surprise and shook his head. "Harvey and my friends have made comments over the years, too. But you've always been too focused on studying to notice any of them."

I continued to regard him skeptically, but he merely shook his head. "I'm just saying I'm not surprised you've caught the eye of this mage boy. That doesn't mean I like it, though. He may be mageborn, but that doesn't give him the right to mess with you—whiling away his summer with flirtation and then dropping you cold once his studies resume."

"It's not like that," I assured him. "We don't do anything but study. And eat," I added conscientiously. "Obviously we also have to eat sometimes. I've made so much progress with my reading and writing. I swear Zak's never even tried to hold my hand."

One of Anson's brows shot up. "Zak?"

I bit my lip at my slip-up, but I didn't break eye contact, not giving an inch.

He sighed again, capitulating to my beseeching expression. "Fine. I won't say anything. But I hope you know what you're doing, Aria."

I grinned. "You always were my favorite brother, Anson!"

"Ha! I heard you telling Timothy the same thing only last week."

I gave him a quick squeeze. "I have a very flexible mind."

I raced out of the alley, wanting to be on my way before he could change his mind. But I slowed down as soon as I was out of sight, my thoughts heavy. Anson's words had reminded me just how dangerous it was to allow myself foolish hope. I needed to focus on my studies for the last weeks of the summer and nothing else.

When I ran into Zak several streets away from the office of sealed affairs, I couldn't greet him with my usual cheer. Constraint gripped me, and it put me on edge. I hated the loss of our old ease.

For his part, he greeted me as usual, falling into step beside me as we made our way toward our shared destination. But as we passed a dark side alley, he took a sudden turn, pulling me after him.

"Let's go this way," he said. "We haven't walked this route yet."

"That's because it stinks," I said testily, eyeing a questionable pile against a side wall.

I glanced back at the street we had just left, trying to spot the reason for his sudden change of direction. It was completely empty.

I came to an abrupt stop, my frustration spilling over. I couldn't bring up the true source of my discomfort, so it had latched on to a new target instead.

"What in the kingdom is going on, Zak? The street's completely empty! There's no one to avoid, so why are we ducking down a stinky alley?"

Zak had stopped several steps further on, taken by surprise, but he returned to me in two quick strides at my words. "That's what you thought I was doing?" he demanded.

I shrugged, regretting my momentary loss of control. "I figured you were avoiding someone you knew. It's not a big deal."

Zak took a step back, his brows knit. "If that were true, it would definitely be a big deal, Aria. Why didn't you say anything? Have you been thinking that all this time?"

He seemed genuinely distressed at my assumption, but if it hadn't been for that reason, I couldn't think of any other.

"If not that, then why?" I asked. "Are you some secret inspector, tasked with inspecting every back alley of Corrin?" I tried to make my words light and amused, but my tone fell flat.

"I—" Zak looked away, running a hand through his hair. He groaned. "I was trying to lure out the Shrouded Killer. You said once that I fit the profile of his victims, and I agree. I thought that if I came to his notice, he might choose me as his next target."

"WHAT?!" I shouted so loudly that two startled birds took flight from the next alley over. I lowered my voice. "You've been doing *what*?"

He grimaced guiltily, and I shook my head. "No, wait. Not here." Grabbing his arm, I towed him behind me at my fastest walk, hustling us both into the office of sealed affairs and into the first empty study room I found. Closing the door firmly behind us, I turned to face him, my arms crossed.

I still remembered how he had responded when I told him he looked like one of the Shrouded Mage's victims. He had seemed pleased and excited, which had confused me at the time, although I hadn't thought of it since. What in the kingdom was going on in his brain?

He watched me, his expression chagrined. And when I didn't immediately speak, he filled the silence.

"I wasn't planning to say anything about it. But if you've been thinking I'm ashamed to be seen with you…I never want you to think that, Aria."

"Do you think this is a better option?" I asked, outraged. "I'd far rather you be ashamed of me than find out you're trying to become the next victim of a serial killer. That's the most outrageous thing I've ever heard. And it doesn't even make sense. They already caught the Shrouded Mage and sealed him. I was there myself! And given how many people he killed, he must have been given a life sentence on top of his sealing. He's currently sitting in a cell somewhere."

Zak winced. "Actually, that wasn't the Shrouded Killer."

"What?" I cried before glancing quickly at the door and lowering my voice.

"Are you serious? They caught the wrong person? How could that happen? And how could you possibly know about it, even if it did?!"

"Not the wrong person, exactly. But not the Shrouded Killer."

"But they sealed him! Are you telling me they sealed an innocent mage by mistake?"

"No, of course not!" he said quickly. "With all the power behind the law enforcement compositions, there's no chance of a mistake like that. Once they have someone in custody, they have compositions to establish the truth."

I lowered myself into the closest chair, shaking my head.

"Nothing you're saying is making sense."

Zak dropped into the next chair over, leaning forward and speaking quickly. "The man who sealed you is a murderer, but he only killed one person. He was one of those copycats I mentioned. He had a grudge against someone, and he took the opportunity to kill them, making it look like a shrouded killing. He misused his power in the worst possible way and deserved his punishment, you don't need to worry about that."

"But..." I stared at him. "But everyone thinks the Shrouded Mage has been caught! If law enforcement knows that isn't true, why haven't they told everyone?"

Zak's lips tightened into a thin line. "Plenty of mages know it. But law enforcement says it's better for the commonborns to think he's been caught. That way we won't have any more copycats."

"But the copycat was a mage!" I protested. "How does it help if the commonborns are the only ones who don't know the truth? People were more careful when they knew the Shrouded Mage was roaming the city, and now they've let their guard down again. My own brothers are at risk from him!"

I stood, and Zak mirrored me. But after a second, I sat back down, and once again he followed me.

"I agree." His voice vibrated with feeling. "But some of the influential merchant families were bringing a lot of pressure to bear on both the crown and the law enforcement discipline over their failure to catch the killer. I think law enforcement is more interested in escaping that pressure than anything else."

"You mean they've given up looking for him?" I gaped at Zak, appalled.

He shook his head. "It isn't as bad as that. They're still looking. But I've always felt they could have assigned more resources to the search, and now they're expending even less effort." His expression turned dark. "If he'd been stalking mageborn youth, it would have been a different story."

"He would have already been caught," I muttered.

Discontented murmurs to that tune had been filling the city in the weeks leading up to the Shrouded Mage's apparent capture. The talk had died down since, attention turning to the unexpected sealing ceremony instead. And that fact only lent weight to Zak's theory.

I narrowed my eyes at him. "I can accept all of that, even if I don't like it. Unfortunately, it sounds all too believable. But none of it explains why you've been wandering around the lower city dressed like a commonborn trying to attract the attention of a violent killer!"

"I can't just sit back and do nothing!" he said. "As mages we have a responsibility to use our power to help all the people of Ardann, not just other mages."

"An admirable view," I said tartly. "But I don't see how getting yourself murdered is using your power to help anyone."

"I never intended to get murdered." His smile only made me narrow my eyes further. "You have no idea how many compositions I have in my jacket right now. The Shrouded Killer hunts weak victims, but if I can come to his notice and lure him into making an attempt on me, he'll find I'm not in the least weak."

"Oh really?" I asked, my voice heavy with irony. "Just like in that alley the first day we met, perhaps?"

Zak winced. "With one opponent it would be different. I wasn't expecting to be jumped by three people at once."

I slumped back against my seat. "There are so many things that could go wrong! What have you been thinking?"

Zak's face tightened, and I caught something sharp and painful lurking in his eyes. I straightened.

"What is it? What aren't you telling me?"

He sighed. "I'm genuinely disgusted by law enforcement's approach to this. I meant everything I said about that. But it's also personal for me."

"Personal?" My brows drew together. "I thought all the victims have been commonborn?"

"They have." His volume dropped. "Do you really think that means it couldn't be personal for me?"

His eyes met mine steadily, his expression laden. My gaze slid away, and I swallowed, unwilling to consider the meaning of the look that filled his eyes.

"So you knew one of the victims?" I asked instead, trying to work out how that could have happened.

But he shook his head. "Not directly." When I frowned, he hurried on. "One of the victims was the son of a cousin of someone I know."

I tried to follow his words, skeptical of what sounded like a very tenuous connection.

His fist clenched and then unclenched, his expression growing pained. "We've talked about our families, so you know my parents are academics. That's why they're so determined for me to follow their footsteps into the University. They love me well enough, and of course I love them, but..."

He looked up with a ghost of his usual smile. "They weren't always very present. If they weren't physically at either the University or palace library, they were often lost to abstraction. So I was raised more by the servants than I was by them. Our housekeeper's daughter took on the role of my nanny, and she's always been a second mother to me. It's her cousin who lost his son to the Shrouded Killer. She's not needed as a nanny anymore, but of course she still works for our family. Normally she lives at our family's home here in Corrin, but she took two whole months off to stay with her cousin and his wife after it happened."

"And law enforcement hasn't been doing enough to find the killer," I said slowly, a number of things making more sense—including why Zak was so comfortable among commonborns. "So you thought you'd chase him down yourself."

"Not quite that," Zak said with a wince. "Nanny made me promise that I wouldn't." He grinned. "She knows me too well."

I raised a brow.

"I swore I wouldn't do anything to search for him," Zak said quickly in response. "And I haven't. But if he were to happen to find me..."

"That seems like a hair-fine distinction," I said dryly, relieved that he'd been constrained from doing anything more active.

"And now you're going to make me promise to stop

even that," he said dejectedly. "I just wish there was something I could do to help properly."

"Apparently you're the only one who feels that way among the mages," I said sourly.

"I know there are others who care," he said with feeling, his whole bearing becoming more animated. "But it's criminal the way so many mages ignore the plight of the commonborn. Times are changing now that we have sealing ceremonies, but they could be changing faster. At the very least, we should be running things more efficiently."

I hid a smile. He always got swept up in enthusiasm whenever his talk turned to systems that could be more efficient.

"Take your situation." A martial light came into his eyes. "Your teacher should never have had the power to overlook you in favor of someone more valuable to him personally. If it happened to you—twice!—it's probably happening in schools all over the kingdom."

He didn't slow down, properly worked up now. "And taking the top student from each school doesn't make sense. Of course we need to spread out the places and make sure some are chosen from all regions of Ardann, but what if one school has two brilliant students and another has none? We need a more centralized system, and one with better oversight."

My lips twitched, but I nodded. "I agree. How do you think it should be run, then?"

He frowned thoughtfully. "I would need to think about it more, to make sure I covered every possible angle, but I think the advanced schools shouldn't cover a full eight years. At some earlier age—sixteen maybe? Or fourteen might be better?—local schooling should finish and teachers should refer all their best students to further training in a centralized location."

"Here in Corrin?" I asked, fascinated by the idea.

"That would make most sense," he agreed. "And students should have a choice, too, about which stream they want to enter. There's already a teaching college, so students could choose whether they go there or to the University."

"Or to one of the merchant companies," I interjected, and he nodded.

"There may even be other options. The nominated students in each stream could be trained together, and during that time, their trainers could weed out anyone who didn't prove suitable after all. Then those who made it all the way through the extra training would be sealed and progress to their chosen career."

I considered his suggestion. "That would be a good system," I agreed. "Much better than the current one anyway. I know you were only a trainee until a couple of months ago, but have you suggested it to your parents? Maybe they could put the idea forward on your behalf?"

He snorted. "I've talked to them about it, but they just took it as an opportunity to push my joining the University. They say that if I make it through a university course, I can become a royal official and make all these changes I'm so enthusiastic about."

"At the risk of agreeing with your parents on anything," I said with fake meekness, "that's actually a good suggestion."

"But I would have to study at the University for years!" Zak cried. "Can you imagine it?"

"Actually I can. When you're interested in the topic, you do quite well with your study."

"It's a fairly significant caveat," he muttered, but I shook my head.

"You would be a much better official than most of the current ones. I'm sure of it." My voice turned stern. "But not if you get murdered before you even make it to the University."

He closed his eyes, taking a breath before opening them again. "Is it really doing much harm for me to wander around the lower city dressed like a commonborn?" He gave me his most charming look. "Especially if I have you with me. If the Shrouded Killer proved too much for me, I'm sure you would rescue me as easily as you did last time."

I snorted, but I knew him well enough to know that he must have utter faith in his arsenal of compositions. He wouldn't have put me at risk by walking around the city in my company otherwise. Although he was probably expecting that if the Shrouded Mage noticed him, he would attack later, when Zak was alone. So far, the Shrouded Mage had always attacked lone victims, and always males.

Personally, I put more faith in the unlikeliness of the killer targeting Zak when he had so many potential victims. And that reassurance galvanized me into one of my occasional bouts of recklessness.

"As long as you only wander off well-used roads when you're with me," I declared.

I had been studying so relentlessly that I welcomed a small thrill in my days—even if it was only playing with danger and not truly taking any risks.

Zak laughed delightedly. "I think you might be the only person I know who would say that."

"Careful, or you'll convince me I'm being foolish," I said with a warning look. "I'm already aware I should be joining the general chorus and telling you not to make yourself bait for a serial killer. You make me sound like the only friend who wishes you ill."

Zak grinned. "You love me too. You know it."

I coughed, turning quickly away from him. He had spoken without thinking, and I couldn't let him see how much his words had affected me.

He jumped to his feet. "I'll go get our things from our locker."

He disappeared from the room, leaving me to my frantic recovery attempts.

Ducking into every suspicious alley we saw turned out to be more fun than I was expecting. I didn't think for a second that we would actually find the Shrouded Mage lurking down any of them. Privately I thought he'd ended his killing spree for good, taking the exit provided by his copycat. It galled me to think he might go free as a consequence, but I could only be glad for the continued absence of any new victims.

But despite the lack of any real danger, Zak and I crept around like intelligencers on a mission for our kingdom, and the camaraderie was heady. When Zak looked at me, a gleam in his eyes as he silently invited me to partner with him, I couldn't help following him anywhere he went.

Summer was drawing to a close, however, and our days spent in the lower city would end with it. We were both bound for the University in autumn, and that meant various preparations were needed beyond our usual studies. Unlike the commonborn students, the mage students lived at the University for the years of their study, and Zak had more to do in preparation than me.

As the summer wound down, I had several days to myself, and without Zak to keep me company, I couldn't bring myself to stay shut up in a study room. Instead, my feet drew me toward the largest of the lower city's markets —a bustling place that I usually avoided in favor of the quieter ones nearer home. When I was absorbed in study, I didn't have the patience for navigating large crowds.

The noise of the market soon lifted my spirits, however, the energy of the place proving catching. I wandered between the stalls, admiring the wares and thinking about which food stalls I would have liked to patronize if I only had some coin in my pocket.

"Aria!" The unexpected voice set off a flood of emotion. Even after two years, I recognized it instantly.

I turned slowly to face Gina. She pushed through the crowd toward me, her face alight.

She looked just as she always had—the tight curls of her dark hair springing wildly in all directions. The fine material and elegant cut of her dress were at odds with the crooked way she wore it, as if she'd pulled it on in a rush and not taken time to look in a mirror. The familiarity of the details made my stomach clench.

She was still the same Gina. And yet the Gina I had known would never have betrayed me.

She hurried the final steps to stand in front of me, her smile faltering as she took in my expression. Hesitating, she glanced at the crowd around us, frowning as someone bumped her, making her stumble closer to me.

"Come on! Over here!" Grasping my wrist, she pulled

me between two stalls, moving us out of the flow of the market crowd.

My feet followed reluctantly, although I could have easily pulled free. Hurt pulsed inside me, but even stronger was the desire to look her in the face and ask her why she had done it.

"Aria, I just heard the news!" she cried as soon as she came to a stop. "You've been sealed!"

She looked so genuinely delighted that I didn't know what to say. Had it really taken her all summer to hear?

"I just got back from the Sekali Empire yesterday," she added, clearing up that question.

The information didn't do anything to assuage my resentment, however. Gina was a Robart and had already been sealed for two years, so of course she had been given the opportunity to travel to the Empire with Faylee. Being sealed in my place had opened up a lifetime of possibilities for her.

"How fortunate for you," I said stiffly. "It must have been an incredible experience."

"Yes, yes, but never mind that!" she said in her old breathless style. "I was furious when I heard Byron managed to get himself sealed—he's a worse student than me and I was never top of the class—but then someone said you'd been sealed as well."

I wanted to lash out at her. If she'd accosted me three months ago, I would have. But the situation had grown complicated. The Robarts were the ones who had denied me my rightful place at a sealing ceremony. But Faylee was a Robart, and that meant they had also been the ones to ensure I was sealed in the end.

"It was kind of Faylee to intervene on my behalf," I said quietly. "And very like her."

I gave Gina a significant look, hoping she would read on my face what I wasn't saying with my words. Faylee was different from the rest of the Robarts.

"Was it Faylee who arranged for you to be sealed?" Gina sounded genuinely astonished. "I've been dying to know how you managed it." She grinned. "It does sound like something she would do. I told her all about you two years ago, and she was most displeased with what Father did to get me selected instead of you. She said our family won't succeed in the long term unless we earn a reputation for fair dealing. She's very influential, even with the family elders, so Father was in disgrace for months. And I was so glad to hear she followed my suggestion and actually went to meet you."

I stared at her. "*You* were the one to send Faylee to me?"

Gina nodded, her face falling. She grabbed both my hands, pinning me with an anguished, pleading expression.

"I know I'm the worst sort of coward," she exclaimed. "I should have come to you myself. But I was just so ashamed! I couldn't bear to face you after what I did."

I drew a shaky breath. I wanted to pull my hands free, but seeing her again after so long was like being caught in the fog of the past. Along with my resentment had come a surge of old memories of all the fun we had shared together. I couldn't entirely harden my heart against the genuine emotion in her eyes. Gina had never been one for artifice—which had made her subterfuge and betrayal all the more devastating.

"Not that I did it on purpose," she said earnestly. "I hope you can believe that, Aria. I didn't know anything about it."

Her words made me start and finally pull myself free. But I didn't storm off. A small shoot of hope had unfurled inside my chest, my curiosity driving its growth.

"What do you mean?" I asked.

"Father was always disappointed that I wasn't a better student," she said. "He wanted me to be first in the class, but I never had the temperament for it."

She laughed slightly, and I almost smiled with her before I remembered she had been first—once.

"But before that last test, he suddenly became fierce. He hounded me day and night and said I needed to come first in one test at least. He said if I could just come first in the next test, he would let me breathe again. So I studied my heart out. I still didn't think I was likely to beat you, but then you got sick and—" Her face twisted.

"You truly didn't know why he wanted you to study so hard for that test?" I asked.

She shook her head energetically, her curls bouncing. "Of course not! Or I would have told you too! I was never even particularly eager to go to the University. It just meant four more years of study!" She wrinkled her nose before brightening again. "But it's much better than I'd feared. You're going to love it."

"Never mind that," I said, not ready to think about the future when I was still lost in the past. "If you didn't know before the test, you must have realized after. If you didn't want to steal my place, why did you agree to be sealed?"

"They only told me about it the day before," she said. "And then they insisted on having a celebratory family meal, so I couldn't get out of the house. Of course I protested about being chosen and said the position should have been yours, but they told me the mage being sealed was powerful enough that the school had been allowed to submit two names."

My brows rose, belief worming its way through me. I had never been able to understand how the Gina I had known could have done such a thing. But I had no trouble believing her father might have deceived her too. And that meant Gina hadn't plotted to steal my place from me. She hadn't even known she was stealing it.

"They told me you'd be at the ceremony as well, but it was such a crowd, I couldn't find you. It wasn't until afterward that I realized you were never there, and it was all a lie. But it was too late, then."

"Why didn't you tell me all this two years ago?" I asked, not quite willing to forgive her so easily.

"I should have," Gina said, wilting visibly. "And I know I'm a terrible coward for not doing so. But even if I didn't take your spot knowingly, I still took it, and there was no way for me to make that right. And besides, my family did know what they were doing, even if I didn't. How could you ever look at me the same way again? I hid in the house all summer, and then I started at the University, so we had no reason to cross paths. I…" She grabbed my hands again, squeezing them and wailing, "I'm so sorry for being such an awful friend!"

I drew a long breath. "I wish I'd known this two years ago. I would have been furiously angry, but I think I would have understood and not blamed you."

"And now?" she asked in a small voice. "We're going to

be at the University together after all, even if I'll be two years ahead. I can show you around and introduce you to my friends and—"

She broke off and waited, looking hopefully at my face.

Something tight and dark inside me loosened. The picture she painted was appealing—and not just because of the help she could give as I adjusted to the world of the University. Gina's friendship had made my early years at school fun and bright, despite the study, and now I could have that again as I started at the University.

Just as Zak had started to drift away from me—absent as he made his arrangements for his upcoming new life—Gina had reappeared. I already had one friend at the University, but he was dangerous to me in ways I didn't like to dwell on. Gina represented a much safer friendship, and she could do what Zak couldn't. She could help me settle into the place where I belonged—the commonborn stream.

Gina had wronged me when she cut off our friendship without a word of explanation, but thoughts of Zak reminded me that I was also prone to making foolish, emotional decisions where friendships were concerned. If I always acted rationally myself, I would never have gotten so close to him.

I let out my breath in a sigh of release.

"It's true that your family wronged me, but in the end they also made it right." I held up an arm to show the marks ringing my wrist. "And the wrong wasn't your doing. In fact, if you were the one to send Faylee to me, you're responsible for the situation being mended. Of course I'll forgive you. And I would love to meet your University friends."

She let go of my hands, jumping up and down and clapping, as if we were twelve again.

"It's going to be the most fun!" She pulled me into a crushing embrace.

I spluttered and laughed, my face full of suffocating curls. Wrestling free, I shook my head at her. "Shouldn't two years at the University have sobered you a little?"

She laughed. "Mother says that nothing can do that and that Father should have known better from the start. But my brother never had a chance at coming first in any test, so I was his only hope. Which means he's stuck with me."

A raised voice from the market crowd drew my attention as more voices took up the cry, an excited rustle sweeping through the mass of people. If something had happened to catch the attention of everyone in the market, it must have been big.

"What's going on?" I asked, my voice sharp.

Gina turned to follow the direction of my gaze, apparently not having noticed the change in the crowd. "Someone's calling something. Can you hear what they're saying?"

Without waiting for an answer, she dove into the crowd, and I hurried behind, trying not to lose her. Several steps ahead of me, she accosted a stranger, her face alight with curiosity as she asked what was going on.

"They're saying there's been another killing!" the woman exclaimed, eyes wide.

"*Another* killing?" I asked, reaching their side. "You don't mean another shrouded killing? It was the Shrouded Mage?"

The woman nodded. "That's what they're saying, but it can't be true, can it?" She looked doubtful. "The Reds caught him!"

"I heard that was a copycat," I said, but I hardly heard my own words.

A single, terrible, unendurable thought had caught my mind, making it hard to breathe.

I snatched at the woman's sleeve, ignoring her horrified exclamations in response to my comment. "Where?" I asked urgently. "Did you hear where they found the body?"

"Just beyond the market, I think." She pointed toward one of the market exits—the one that led deeper into the city, toward the area where the mages lived.

I took off running, Gina's cries soon lost behind me. I pushed through the crowd with abandon, slipping under people's arms and even elbowing people aside as needed.

Zak wasn't with me. He was alone today. I wasn't there to save him.

The thoughts ran through my mind on a never-ending loop, growing more and more frantic with each repetition. *I hadn't been there.*

CHAPTER 11

The crowd grew more tumultuous as I approached the exit, shoving and pulling in all directions as some people pushed forward in curiosity while others tried to flee. I was jostled and buffeted on every side, but I didn't stop. Ignoring the protests at my passage, I squirmed through any gap I could find, moving toward the place where the body apparently lay.

I couldn't bear to see it, and yet I was desperate to reach it at the same time. Until I saw the victim with my own eyes, I could still cling to the hope that it wasn't Zak. Foolish Zak who went out of his way to come to the Shrouded Mage's notice.

"What a terrible tragedy," a woman said to another as they moved in the opposite direction. "That poor young man."

"And so handsome and nicely dressed," the other responded, and my heart seized.

The words in my head reduced to a mindless stream. *Nononononononono.*

It was easy to see which side street to turn down, and I burst through a final wall of people, emerging into a small circle of open space. Someone—perhaps a resident of one of the neighboring houses—was kneeling beside the young man with a solemn expression, pulling a sheet over the body.

I leaned forward to get a glimpse of the face before it was covered, but I was too late. Something twisted and writhed in my chest, trying to crawl up my throat. I had to know.

I took a step forward despite the ring of watching eyes, when a voice called my name.

"Aria!"

Spinning, I gasped as my eyes fell on Zak's tall figure. He stood against the wall of a building, as if pushed back as far as possible by the jostling crowd, and his eyes were fixed on me.

I ran toward him, the people between us giving way with unhappy mutters. Concern overlayed the sorrow and anger in Zak's eyes, perhaps in response to my obvious agitation.

Without hesitation, I flung myself into his arms, the overwhelming relief robbing my knees of strength.

"You're alive!" I sobbed out, my words verging on hysterical. "I thought…When I heard they'd found a body, I thought…And I wasn't with you today. You could have come down into the city on your own and…"

His strong arms circled me, holding me tight against him, steady despite my failing legs.

"I'm fine, Aria." His reassuring murmur washed over me. "I wasn't here when it happened. You'd mentioned coming to this market today, so I was heading in this direction when the shouting started. I followed the crowd the rest of the way."

"You're really unharmed?" I sniffed against his chest, and he tightened his hold.

"As you can see."

I tried to draw back so I could get a proper look at him, but he didn't loosen his hold. My gaze jumped to his face, catching there at the expression in his eyes.

"Zak." My voice came out shaky, not yet recovered from the intensity of my panic.

"Aria," he breathed back, his eyes dropping to my lips.

He swayed toward me, and I could think of nothing beyond my all-consuming relief that he was alive and well. I had told myself pretty words about friendship, but what I felt for Zak was much stronger than that, no matter what self-deceptions I employed. Despite all my attempts at caution, I had fallen headlong into love with him.

And the Shrouded Mage hadn't found him. He was alive.

Strength returned to my legs, and I lifted my heels off the ground, closing the distance between us and pressing my lips against his. Fire raced through me as I forgot all about the crowded street or his mage status.

Zak was alive, and he was holding me in his arms.

"Aria!" A furious cry gave me half a second's warning before someone grabbed my arm and ripped me violently away from Zak.

I cried out, stumbling and nearly falling as I was pulled sideways away from his warm grasp. Zak growled, stepping toward us and reaching for me, but I got a look at my attacker.

"Anson!" I gasped, the blood draining from my face. "What are you doing here?"

"Half of Corrin is here." His narrowed eyes didn't leave Zak's face, not even glancing toward the covered body.

"Please, Anson," I pleaded. "You don't understand."

Zak, who had looked ready to wrench me from Anson's grasp, hesitated at the obvious familiarity between us. He threw me a questioning look, and I mouthed the words, *my brother.*

Zak's expression changed, an almost guilty look creeping into his eyes. He cleared his throat and stepped back, giving us space.

"You promised, Aria." Anson's voice was implacable. "I was clearly a fool to trust you."

He dragged me down the street, pausing only briefly as we passed Zak. "Mage or not," he said in a threatening undertone, "don't play with my sister."

"I wasn't—" Zak's attempted response was lost in the noise of the crowd as Anson pulled me inexorably on.

The crowd parted before Anson's angry expression, watching us go with curiosity, although no one attempted to intervene once they got a look at my resigned face. I could have pulled free—they knew it and I knew it. But I was already going to be in big trouble at home, and I didn't want to make it worse.

I'm sorry, I mouthed at Zak over my shoulder, but I wasn't sure if he'd seen me.

As soon as we'd made it through the crowd and were no longer at risk of being separated by the throng, I pulled my arm loose, nearly jogging to keep up with Anson's fast pace.

"It wasn't Zak's fault." My shoulders slumped. "He didn't do anything."

"It looked like he was doing plenty to me," my brother growled.

"It was me." I forced the words out, despite the humiliation sweeping over me. "When I heard there had been another murder, I was terrified it might have been him. When I saw him alive and well, I was so relieved that I...I got carried away." I finished awkwardly.

At the time I had been convinced Zak was leaning toward me—that I was only finishing what he had begun. But walking beside Anson, it was all too easy to believe I had been mistaken. Caught up in overwhelming emotion, I had practically attacked Zak!

"Regardless of who started it, he wasn't exactly pushing you away, was he?" Anson asked caustically, although I thought I detected a hint of softening.

For a moment, his words gave me hope that I hadn't acted alone after all, but a moment's reflection dashed it. "He's far too much of a gentleman to push me away at a moment like that," I said sadly. "I was practically hysterical with fear."

Anson's brow rose. "What happened to only being friends?"

I didn't attempt to reply. What reply could I possibly make?

The scene when we reached home was painful beyond words. News of the latest killing had reached the house ahead of us, so we were initially pounced on for fresh news, everyone exclaiming at once.

But Anson responded brusquely, telling them it had been a Robart—something I hadn't known—before announcing there was something more pressing we needed to discuss. I had been hoping to avoid a full family council, but everyone was home except Harvey, and he arrived two minutes after us, bringing the news of the killing in case we hadn't heard.

All six of them filed into the sitting room, their faces ranging from curious to concerned. But when Anson gave them a brief and unflattering account of my summer with my mage tutor, they responded with a united front.

By the time I finally escaped to my bed after the evening meal, nothing could have been clearer. Mages did not have serious romantic intentions toward common-borns. It was impossible. And I was a fool to throw myself at him. I had only set myself up for heartbreak.

"It could be worse than youthful heartbreak, too," Harvey had said in his measured way. "You say he's a decent enough sort, and I hope you're right. But if he is, he may well feel some measure of shame when his interest moves on. If that happens, he might find it uncomfortable to see you, even in passing, and he might exert influence to make sure you don't cross paths in the future. This could end up limiting your career opportunities."

"He's a minor mage," I said weakly, knowing it would be useless to protest that Zak would never do that. "How much influence can he have if he's spending his time tutoring in the lower city?"

"Even so, he's a mage," my father said. "And he's just

spent four years at the Academy with every mage his age in the kingdom. He moves in circles we don't even understand."

They all thought I had been inexcusably foolish, but even so, they directed their anger toward Zak, their attitude toward me one of concern. It was that loving concern that eventually wore me down until I capitulated to my mother's demands and promised I would stop studying with Zak. I had made enough progress that I could continue my reading practice without him, so I had no excuse to give.

Anson had added that I wasn't to go wandering around the markets with him either. I put up no protest to that final restriction, already having accepted that my summer with Zak was over. Even the weather had turned, and there were only two weeks left until University classes started.

Not that my family could keep me away from him forever. They had to know that I would see him again once we both started at the University.

But they seemed to hope that a period of separation would bring me to my right mind, and that when we were at the University, we would find ourselves in different spheres entirely. Likely they were right.

In the hopes of alleviating my mother's teary self-recriminations for not inspecting Zak for herself before agreeing to our tutoring exchange, I told them about my reconciliation with Gina. That news was greeted with joy, and my mother had soon convinced herself that at the University I would be too busy with Gina and her friends to even notice the mage students.

Lying in my bed, I allowed myself a small, bitter laugh.

If my family thought that two weeks was enough to forget Zak, they were utterly mistaken.

Even with the embarrassment that now overlaid my bold actions, I couldn't help re-living our kiss again and again. Alone in my room, I could feel the pressure of his arms around me and the fire of his lips on mine.

My family didn't know Zak. And they didn't know the strength of my feelings for him. Two weeks wasn't close to enough. They hoped that heartbreak could still be averted, but it was too late for that.

But they had one thing right. Mages didn't marry commonborns, whatever I had told myself about the gap between us shrinking.

The next morning, I rose without looking at myself in the mirror. I didn't want to see the dark circles under my eyes that would proclaim my lack of rest.

I dressed hurriedly, creeping through the house and peering around corners to make sure I escaped the house unseen. I wasn't sure if my family would stop me, but I couldn't risk finding out.

The night before I had promised that I would end my studies with Zak, and even that I wouldn't spend time with him outside the office of sealed affairs. But I couldn't just disappear. They didn't know him like I did, and he would be deeply worried at any unexplained absence. He might even come to our house again.

I shivered at the prospect of that scene. I didn't want my family confronting Zak. And that meant I needed to meet him one more time to explain that I couldn't see him until we started at the University.

I scanned the streets as I jogged through the city, finally

spotting him three streets away from the sandstone building. He greeted me with concern, his eyes assessing my face, and his look of worry growing deeper. I beckoned him down the cleanest-looking alley I could find, and he readily followed. But now that the moment had come, it was hard to find the right words.

"I can't study with you anymore," I finally blurted out.

His brows drew together. "Why not? We still have two weeks before classes—"

"I promised my family," I said miserably, unable to meet his eyes. "It's only for two more weeks, so you shouldn't be disadvantaged by it…" I trailed off, unable to think of any explanation that wouldn't be insulting to him.

My family had misunderstood Zak's nature, attributing ill intent toward him that I couldn't speak out loud. And neither could I confess the humiliating truth about my own feelings or my understanding of the impossibility of his ever returning them in any serious way.

"Is this because I kissed you?" he asked. "Because I—"

"You mean I kissed you," I said quickly, my cheeks warming. "I explained that to my brother. It wasn't your fault."

Zak's brows rose. "Fault?"

"I don't want to talk about it," I said hurriedly, my face now flaming.

He stepped closer, reaching out a concerned hand. "Aria, I—"

I took a swift step back, and his hand dropped.

"I've made my family a promise. And like I said, we're only missing two weeks. I can read well enough to practice on my own now, and you've made a lot of progress, too.

I'm sure you'll do fine once classes start. And once we're at the University, we can—" I hesitated. "We can see each other again there. If we find we want to. I actually met Gina in the market yesterday—my old Robart friend who was sealed instead of me. She apologized, and she's going to show me around the University and introduce me to her friends."

Zak continued to watch me with knit brows, but I needed him to know that I had other friends. I would be all right at the University, even without him. I didn't want him to feel guilted into anything.

And there was something else I needed from him too.

"I need you to make me a promise," I said, and he answered quickly.

"Anything."

I swallowed. It was an alluring statement.

But I could see the concern in his eyes. He was worried about me, and I wasn't going to take advantage of that. Except for one thing. Where one matter was concerned, I would take ruthless advantage of his opening.

"Good," I said resolutely. "Then I'll already take your promise as given. You have to stop looking for the Shrouded Mage."

His eyes widened, but I held up my hand to forestall his words. "Or whatever you want to call him. You have to stop trying to lure him out and forget about him entirely. Now that we're no longer meeting, you shouldn't have any reason to even come into the lower city."

"But Aria, he's just killed again. It's more important than ever that—"

"That the Reds track him down," I said loudly over the

top of him. "I quite agree." I gave him my most steely look. "You said you would promise me anything."

He slumped, the fight going out of him, and I wished I felt even a little victorious. But there was nothing in this situation to celebrate.

"Very well, then," he said before looking back up with a spark of defiance. "For two weeks at least. Everything starts fresh when our University classes begin."

I closed my eyes, breathing deeply. My track record of resisting Zak was low, but I would just have to find an inner reserve of strength before then. For now, I would take what I could.

I opened my eyes again, catching a flash of movement from deeper in the alley. I peered after it but couldn't make anything out. If I was fortunate, it had only been a cat and there had been no one to overhear our embarrassing conversation. If someone had heard, though...I shivered. I needed to get away as quickly as possible before I ended up humiliating myself further.

Somehow I dredged up a smile. "Two weeks free of study. I hope you enjoy them."

"Just two weeks," Zak said, as if responding to something else entirely. "And then we make a fresh start."

I nodded once and fled out of the alley, telling myself as I went that it was merely a strategic retreat.

CHAPTER 12

The two weeks before classes felt longer than the two months that had preceded them. Only one thing prevented them from becoming unalleviated misery.

Gina visited, bringing first a cake and then a basket of fresh produce for my mother. My family accepted her gifts as the token of apology that they were, welcoming her back with open arms.

My old friend—now new again—insisted on dragging me out of the house, taking me shopping for everything she assured me I would need. The commonborn students at the University didn't wear black mage robes, of course, but we had our own uniform of sorts, apparently. I wasn't entirely sure if it was officially required, or something adopted more informally by the students, but either way I was eager not to stand out.

Gina told me tales of the lessons and the lecturers and the enormous library that dwarfed the one at the office of sealed affairs.

"They've been building the commonborn one for five

years," she told me. "But the academics have been building the one at the University for five centuries."

"Five hundred years," I said faintly, shaking my head. "I can't imagine how many books it must contain."

"It's awe-inspiring at first," she agreed. "But once classes start, you'll find it a pit of bleak despair instead."

I laughed at her outrageous statement. "I could never."

She grinned impishly. "True, maybe you couldn't. But you wouldn't believe just how many of those books the teachers want us to read!" She gave me an inquiring look. "I assume you've been practicing reading?"

I nodded, and she looked relieved.

"Of course you have. I couldn't doubt it. And I'm sure you picked it up far faster than me. I was in despair in the last few weeks before classes started, but look at you—carefree!"

She didn't quite meet my eyes when she said it, and I knew she'd picked up that there was something wrong. But it would take time to build up the trust that had once existed between us, and she didn't press me for answers.

When the first day of the university year finally arrived, my mother fussed over me for so long that I was half an hour late leaving the house. Thankfully, I had been planning on arriving extremely early, my nerves too tightly strung for me to have any interest lingering in bed.

It wasn't my first time trekking through the city to the white marble walls that surrounded the University grounds. In past years I had gone just to gaze at them and dream of the future. But this section of the city—in the shadow of the palace itself—still felt foreign and unfamiliar as I made the walk on tremulous legs.

On those past occasions, the great, ornate University gates had been closed. A smaller door, cut into the gate itself, had allowed the foot traffic of the day to pass in and out. But on the first day of classes for the year, the gates stood open, welcoming the crowds of returning students.

As I stood in front of the open gates, the nerves which had chased me all the way from the lower city suddenly broke. My four brothers had attended school for differing amounts of time, but each of them had left eventually to take the role waiting for them in my father's business. But I had known from the moment I first left school at age ten that I didn't belong there. I had earned my place at the University through years of hard work, and waiting inside those walls was a library too vast to imagine, with all the knowledge I had ever dreamed of uncovering. I had finally arrived where I belonged.

I stepped confidently through the gateway, looking with curiosity at a black-robed young woman who entered only a step behind me. She paid me no heed, calling instead to a small clump of robed students just inside the gate. They greeted her enthusiastically, and I tried to guess if they were returning students or new Academy graduates, starting at the University for the first time like me.

My eyes didn't linger on them long, however, drawn to the grand scene beyond them, so different from my section of the city. Imposing buildings soared above me, connected with arched walkways. But between the buildings and the gates stretched a vast courtyard featuring three elaborate fountains, their splashing water a soft background to the conversations that filled the air.

I had barely taken it all in before a voice called my

name. I turned toward Gina's excited shout with a smile already on my lips. She had offered to walk to the University with me, but I had wanted to make the journey alone on my first day—as I had firmly told all four of my brothers and my mother at least three times. But now that I had arrived, I was glad to see a friendly face. The University was enormous, and I had no idea where to go now that I was inside its grounds.

Gina dashed toward me and seized my arm, chattering happily as she dragged me over to a group of clustered students. As she had promised, they all wore outfits that matched my own new one, and I was grateful for her guidance.

"This is my oldest friend, Aria," Gina announced to the group. "She should have been sealed with me, but she didn't end up getting a place until the recent ceremony. So even though she's two years behind, she's far smarter than me and will no doubt surpass me almost immediately."

A chuckle swept around the other students at her words, so clearly Gina was well known among them.

"You got sealed in the end," a tall girl said, "and that's what matters. I'm Bea. Feel free to stick close to us today. I still remember my first day far too vividly." She shivered dramatically. "My family lives way down south, near Abalene, and I found Corrin totally overwhelming. You should have seen me when I first came up for my sealing ceremony."

"Me too!" another girl agreed. "And then when the Spoken Mage appeared at the end of the sealing ceremony, I thought I might faint."

"She actually spoke to me," I said. "We had a conversation about our brothers—and then I got out of the building and discovered I still had breakfast in my hair."

Every one of the girls made dismayed noises of sympathy.

"I can remember my ceremony as clearly as if it was yesterday," one of the boys said. "I was terrified I was going to have to say something, totally convinced I was going to mess it up. But of course I didn't have to do anything at all. I couldn't have messed it up if I tried."

"Unless you missed it altogether," I said dryly, recounting my own near miss and desperate sprint through the city.

Gasps of horror accompanied my tale, along with a few laughs as I described my bedraggled state and utter relief when I arrived, despite the disapproval of the official.

"I can't believe no one told you!" the tall girl said. "What a disaster it could have been."

"Oh, that reminds me!" Gina cried. "We have a mystery on our hands. I talked to Faylee, and she said she wasn't the one to get your name on the list, although she was delighted when she heard you were included."

"It wasn't Faylee?" I stared at her blankly. "But I don't know anyone else with that kind of influence."

"Like I said—a mystery." Gina's eyes shone. She loved mysteries.

I shook my head, utterly bewildered. I couldn't thank my mysterious benefactor if I didn't know who they were.

My eyes fell on two black-robed students entering the courtyard from one of the arched walkways. As I watched, one waved to the other and disappeared back toward the building, leaving the remaining student to cut across a corner of the courtyard alone, his focus on the building in front of him. As he turned, his face came into view, and a smile broke over my face.

It had only been two weeks since I had last seen Zak, and I wasn't prepared for the wave of joy that crashed over me at sight of his familiar face.

"It's Zak!" I said. "I need to catch him."

I broke away from Gina's group. "Zak!" I called as I half ran toward him, trying to catch him before he exited the courtyard.

My path took me past the group of black-robed students I had seen when I first arrived. They broke off their conversation at my cry, turning to look at me. The girl, who had barely glanced at me before, examined me closely this time, her gaze flicking between me and Zak.

"*You* know Zakary of Callinos?" she asked loudly.

"Zak always did have odd friends," one of her companions said dismissively.

"Even so," another girl tittered.

My steps faltered, my attention wrenched from Zak's distant figure to the closer group of students. Behind me, murmurs broke out among the commonborn students I'd just left.

I glanced back at them to see Bea watching me curiously. The boy beside her leaned toward Gina.

"That's Zakary of Callinos? I've heard of him. His mother was that Callinos lecturer who took our class for that lecture series last year, remember? He's supposed to be very powerful."

"She called him Zak!" Bea said. "She must know him."

She looked inquiringly toward Gina, but Gina only shrugged, her own gaze flashing curiously to me.

My entire body flushed hot and then cold.

Zak was a *Callinos*? Not a minor mage as I had always assumed, but the powerful son of one of the four great mage families who ruled Ardann and controlled the ten mage disciplines.

At times I had dared to imagine that the gap between us wasn't so very large, but I had been completely wrong. Mages valued strength and power above all else, and they carefully guarded the bloodlines that ensured it. A yawning gulf of power and history stood between us.

My feet started moving while my mind was still in chaos. I needed to get away from the whispers and the exclamations and the many watching eyes.

But I had been facing toward Zak, and when I ran, my feet took me too close to him. I was aiming for one of the walkways, planning to pass beneath the arches, cutting across the walkway to whatever lay behind the University buildings. But Zak caught sight of me as I ran.

"Aria!" he called, his voice glad, and I heard a fresh wave of murmurs behind me.

I didn't turn, ignoring his call and urging my feet to run faster. I needed to get out of sight.

It was the only thought I could manage. Once I was alone, I could try to process the enormous, terrible news I had just received.

But running footsteps sounded behind me. When I darted through the walkway and rounded the corner of the building, I wasn't alone.

A park spread out behind the University, softening the stone of the building with its greenery. I plunged into the closest stand of trees, finding a small clearing at its center with yet another fountain.

"Aria!" Zak sounded slightly out of breath as he followed me into the trees. "Why are you running?"

I finally came to a stop, my breath heaving as I spun to look at him. But the words of dismay and recrimination on my lips died at the sight of his handsome face, lined with concern as he waited for my answer. Longing rose up in me, more potent than ever now that I knew, without a doubt, that a truly insuperable barrier lay between us.

Zak's expression changed as he took in mine, a blazing light coming into his eyes.

"You did this first," he said in a throaty murmur. "Now it's my turn."

With two long strides he reached me, his strong arms seizing me around the waist and pulling me against his chest. One of his hands slid up to cradle the back of my head, tilting my face toward him as his lips came down over mine.

The fire from our last kiss sprang instantly back into being as I melted into his embrace, all thoughts driven from my mind. My hands reached up to twine around his neck, and he made a low noise in his throat, breaking off the kiss only to tilt his head and press his lips to mine again.

My knees trembled, and I clung to him, returning his kiss with equal passion, reality forgotten before the strength of our shared emotion. But a sudden thought sprang into my mind, fully formed, and it was enough to make me break away, pushing myself free as I stumbled backward, panting and staring at him with wide eyes.

"It was you!" I said.

"What?" He sounded dazed, his eyes only slowly coming into focus.

"You were the one who got my name added to the list for the sealing ceremony."

His gaze snapped to my face, his eyes instantly alert.

"I thought you were from a minor mage family," I continued, "so it never occurred to me you would have the influence to do it. But you're not a minor mage. You're a Callinos."

He rubbed the back of his neck. "Yes, I'm a Callinos. But I never meant—"

"Don't try to claim you didn't know I'd mistaken your identity," I snapped, the enormity of it all once more at the front of my mind. "All those times you talked about your family. You must have chosen your words and stories with care so as not to give yourself away. If I'd known more about mage society, I would have worked it out anyway. But I was such a fool."

I ran a hand down my face. "You had a housekeeper and a nanny and a whole team of servants besides. How could I have thought you were from a poorer family?"

"I didn't want to put more barriers between us." He stepped forward and tried to take my hand, but I stepped quickly back out of his reach.

"I never lied," he said quickly. "Everything I told you was true. But it's also true that I didn't clarify my family's standing or correct your assumptions about it. I didn't want to."

"But how could you, Zak?" Tears sprang to my eyes.

"I was going to tell you once we started here," he said, his earlier fire extinguished. "I didn't expect you to hear it from someone else the moment you stepped through the gate." He watched me, his gaze worried. "But does it matter so much? It doesn't make a difference to me."

"How can you say that?" I cried. "Of course it makes a difference. Don't you know how easy you are to love, Zak?"

He sucked in a breath at the word love, his face lighting up again.

"You love me? I hoped after that last day near the market, but then you cut off all contact and wouldn't talk about it. I was afraid—"

"Of course I'm in love with you," I said bitterly. "And I'm going to end up with my heart ripped into shreds because there's no possible future for us."

He stepped toward me again, this time firmly taking my hand.

"Says who?" His voice was low and fierce. "I may be a Callinos, but I'm not royalty. There are no laws about who I have to marry."

I gave a sour laugh. "But you're not going to marry a commonborn."

"Why not?" he demanded. "When you leaped into the alley with a war cry, you leaped straight into my heart as well. I've spent the last four years at the Academy with every other mageborn my age in the entire kingdom, and there's not a one of them I prefer to you."

His free hand came up to cup my face, and my treacherous body froze, unable to pull away from his gentle touch and the look in his eyes.

"Do you have any idea how beautiful you are?" he murmured. "Or how incredible your mind is? I grew up around intelligent people, but you're nothing like my parents. Your mind isn't a barrier between you and others, like it is for them—as if they're operating on a different plane from the rest of us. I was a deficient student as much to spite them as anything else, but you made study come alive for me. You opened up your mind and let me into the world of wonder that you see when you learn something new. It was intoxicating."

His voice dropped to a whisper, and he swayed toward me. "You're intoxicating, Aria."

I forced myself to pull from his grip and step back.

"I'm not denying that you feel something toward me." My voice shook slightly.

Zak shook his head stubbornly. "I love you, Aria. That's what I feel."

I shook my head as well. "We've been living in a bubble this summer, Zak. But now we're stepping out into the broader world. And I've already had a taste of how odd other people think it is for us to even be friends, let alone something more."

"I don't care about other people."

"That's easy to say now," I snapped, trying to rein in the storm of emotions making me dizzy. "But how long will your love last if your peers ostracize and snub you? Will any discipline head even accept you into their discipline with me weighing you down? They'll see me as proof that you have poor judgment and a weak mind, however strong your power."

He laughed. "Three of the discipline heads are cousins, and one is my aunt. They won't find me so easy to overlook."

I groaned. "Do you even hear yourself? That makes it worse! What do you think my life will be like at your side?"

"Then we'll go to my family's country estate when we finish at the University," he said, immediately changing tack. "My parents never go there because it's too far from any of their precious libraries. We can make our own life far from the court and the center of power. I don't care about any of that compared to being with you. We can remain betrothed for a year, or two—or our whole studies if that's how long it takes for me to win over our families. I'd marry you tomorrow if I could, but I'll wait as long as it takes just as long as I know I'll get to marry you at the end of it and keep you at my side forever."

He looked at me with hungry eyes, and I fell back another step.

"Our families." The words came out shaky. "What are they going to say? I'm sure you can charm my family into agreeing. Once they know you're serious..." I shook my head, imagining just how excited they would be about my unimaginable leap in status. "But what about your parents? They'll never consent to you marrying a commonborn girl without any power at all, and you clearly care what they think, or you wouldn't be here at all."

"You're forgetting why I agreed to come here in the first place." Zak's voice was serious, his eyes on me. "For most of my time at the Academy, I had no intention of acquiescing and coming to the University. I only agreed to come after I met you. If you remember, I said I was gathering my parents' goodwill for a time in the future when I would have need of it. This is that time."

"All the way back then?" I asked in a choked whisper, temporarily robbed of breath.

"I already told you." He didn't look away. "You began ensnaring me the moment you leaped into my life."

His words were beguiling. I wanted to let myself sway toward him—to have his arms around me again as he made me forget all my objections. But I couldn't believe in his assurances about the future. The divide between us was too firmly entrenched. Who were we to defy all of Ardannian society and its entire history?

If he truly didn't care about his own future or the contempt of his peers, surely he cared about his future children. My cheeks flushed at the thought of bringing up the subject, but I forced myself to say the words.

"Let's say we did get married," I whispered. "What about our future children? Don't you care about them and how they would be viewed by their peers? Don't you think they would resent you for making them weak?"

"Who said they'd be weak?" he asked, with more fire than the question warranted.

I stared at him. "Everyone knows that mages cultivate their bloodlines for strength. Strong mages marry other strong mages so that their children are stronger still. It's how the great families have ensured their power through centuries. It's why royals can only marry other royals or members of a great family."

"Actually, I heard that law is being repealed," he said

quickly. "The Spoken Mage insisted on it. And look at everything else that's happening in the kingdom because of her arrival. Times are changing. By the time our children are adults, Ardann will be a different kingdom."

"I can't believe it will be that different," I whispered.

"I've actually been thinking about the issue of our children," he said, making me blush again. He didn't seem to notice, though, continuing on with enthusiasm. "I knew it would be one of my parents' major objections, so I wanted to have an answer ready. If I want my children to be more powerful than me, I would need to marry another strong mage—to combine strength with strength. That makes sense. But the idea that if I marry a commonborn, my children would be guaranteed only weak control of power is just an assumption. No one has ever actually trialed it."

I frowned. "I thought there had been a few disastrous marriages between a mage and a commonborn in the past, and their children ended up failing the Academy. I thought those examples are why mages are so opposed to the idea."

"True, there have been occasional mages who married commonborns," he said, his enthusiasm not diminished. "But only weak mages from minor families have ever done it. It's true their children were weak, and everyone blamed the commonborn parent. But I'm not convinced. I think children of a mage and a commonborn will have every chance of inheriting a similar level of power to their mage parent. They won't get an advantage of greater strength, but neither is there any reason to think they'll be significantly weaker. And in our case, I have plenty of strength to give our children a good future." He said the words simply, without pride. Just stating a fact.

"I—" I stared at him. "But if you're wrong, we won't know it until it's much too late."

"I'm willing to take that risk, Aria," he said. "I don't care about any of that. The only reason I considered the matter at all is because of my parents." His face softened. "I care about our future children, of course." His voice dropped again. "But just think how incredible they would be, Aria. With your beauty and mind and my power, I defy anyone in Ardann not to love them."

I choked, unable to meet his eyes when he looked at me like that. But I couldn't trust my response. I couldn't trust the emotions that drove both of us. Emotions faded. I had seen enough of life to know that. Without a sturdy foundation, a relationship built on nothing but emotion would never last. And while my status would be forever lifted by our marriage, Zak would be dragged down. If the emotions faded, I would still be elevated, but he would be left with nothing. I couldn't do that to him.

I took two rapid steps back, shaking my head.

"You said we would have a fresh start at the University, Aria," he pleaded. "This is the fresh start I want. Friendship with you isn't enough."

"Yes, we do need a fresh start," I said, but my voice and face didn't offer any hope. "In the lower city, we were tutor and student. Here you're a mage and I'm a commonborn. We'll be in different subjects and different spheres, and we each need to keep to our own people."

"Aria, I can't accept that." His voice had turned desperate. "You said you loved me."

"I do," I whispered. "And that's why I'm not going to do this to you."

He called my name again, but I was already walking away, and I didn't look back.

I somehow held the tears in, and I was glad of it when I got back into the courtyard. Gina and her friends were still waiting for me, clearly driven by curiosity.

I told them shortly that Zak was a tutor I'd once worked with, but that I didn't expect to see much of him at the University. I could see I hadn't entirely assuaged their interest—they knew he was a Callinos, and therefore not the sort of mage who generally tutored—but they had no choice but to accept my words. Gina's eyes clearly signaled she wouldn't be as easy to placate, but she wouldn't press me further until we were alone, so I had time to think of what to say.

A headache was building behind my temples, however, and I barely made it through the first day of classes. When we had a break for the midday meal, Gina took one look at my face and suggested we eat our meal by one of the fountains. She had previously promised she would take me to see the library in our first break, but I was grateful for her forbearance. The day felt heavy and long, and I wasn't in the right headspace for my first glimpse of the library.

Thankfully, my classes had mostly been introductory lectures, and none of the lecturers had called on me to say anything. The others in my first year class might have thought me odd and silent, but I still had Gina to keep me company while I ate.

When I finally stepped out of the University at the end of the day, I felt nothing but relief—a stark contrast to my emotions on arrival. My family had warned me that my connection with Zak would end up spilling over into other areas of my life, and they were already being proved right.

I walked slowly down the street, in no hurry to arrive home and face my family's eager questions. I had no hope of mustering the expected enthusiasm, and my mother would hound me to know why. Not that I meant to tell them the truth. I couldn't even imagine how they would react.

A figure stepped abruptly in front of me, blocking my way so suddenly that I collided with his chest. I bounced back, the words of protest on my lips dying as soon as I got a look at the face in front of me.

Zak grinned down at me. "You're starting to make a habit of that."

I narrowed my eyes at him, but I didn't even know where to start.

"What are you doing?" I finally asked, my voice heavy with weariness. "Have you been following me? Wasn't I clear enough this morning?"

"Crystal clear." His eyes twinkled at me. "While we're inside the University, I'm a mage and you're a commonborn, and we don't cross paths." He gestured around us, grinning. "But we're not in the University."

I groaned. "That's not what I meant, and you know it."

"Perhaps so, but I meant what I said too." His voice turned serious. "I won't let you turn away from us because you're afraid. Especially not if your fear is for me. I've already decided the best thing for my future, and it's you."

His certainty robbed me of words. How could he be so sure?

Someone brushed past us, the sack over his shoulder whacking against my side. Zak frowned after the man, his arm reaching out in a protective fashion to hover beside me.

"Come down here. We can't talk in the street like this." He ushered me into the closest alleyway.

"There's nothing left to talk about," I said, but the words lacked conviction, even in my own ears, and I didn't step past him to return to the street.

"We don't have to talk about us," he said cheerily. "We can talk about your first day if you prefer. Did you enjoy your classes? Did you see the library?"

"I wasn't in the right mood for it," I said shortly.

A brief shadow crossed his eyes, but he quickly smiled. "Does that mean there's still a chance I can be the one to show it to you?"

I couldn't help the small smile that crept up my face. He was irrepressible.

A shadow fell across him from behind, obscuring much of the light. I peered over his shoulder, taking an instinctive step back from the enormous man who blocked the mouth of the alley. He didn't speak, but I thought his hands moved, although it was hard to see what he was doing with Zak standing between us.

Zak frowned, and I expected him to turn to follow my gaze, but my ears caught a faint tearing sound and Zak's eyes widened. He remained in place, making no attempt to turn, despite the increasing terror on my face.

"I heard you've been looking for me," the man said in a low, hissing voice. "You may regret finding me."

The man strolled forward into the alley, and still Zak didn't move. Comprehension finally hit me. The tearing I had heard had been the attacker working a composition—one that must have been designed to hold Zak in place.

A terrible certainty came over me. Was this the way he had incapacitated his previous victims? According to the rumors, none of the victims had shown any sign of defensive wounds.

I screamed, the sound ripped from my throat, but no one came running, the noise apparently lost in the rumble of South Road. The Shrouded Mage turned to me, though, lowering the hood of his robe. I braced myself for the sight of his face, but it was covered in layers of material, leaving only his eyes showing.

"Commonborn," he said in a tone of dismissal that sent a shiver from my head to my toes.

The single word carried a wealth of meaning. It wasn't just an assessment of my lack of power in the situation. This sinister man saw me as less than human—a bug that he would grind beneath his boot merely because it crossed his path.

He turned back to Zak, speaking in a conversational tone that was somehow even more chilling than his previous words. "I wondered if I would be able to do it when the time came. Murder is no small thing. But now that I'm here, I can see how easy it will be."

I swallowed. His words did nothing to dissuade me about his identity—rather, they confirmed my earlier impression. He didn't consider any of his previous killings to be murder. To the Shrouded Mage, killing Zak—a mage-born—would be his first.

Zak's frantic eyes were fixed on me, and I knew with an equal certainty that all his fear was for me. He had promised to protect me, but we had been caught by surprise, and all his compositions were useless if he couldn't use his arms.

Just as had happened at our first meeting. The memory of that occasion flashed into my mind with perfect clarity, and I knew what I had to do.

I had been backing slowly away from our attacker, moving further down the alley, but without pausing to consider, I changed course. Throwing myself forward at full speed, I sprinted the few steps toward Zak.

I didn't try to slow myself as I approached him. Throwing my arms around him, I cushioned the back of his head as the full force of my speeding body hit him, sending us both flying backward onto the cobblestones.

He fell, stiff and straight as a board, caught in the bonds of the Shrouded Mage's composition. I winced as pain jarred up my arms. The rest of Zak's body would be feeling the same pain, but his head was the most important. All that mattered was keeping him alive.

I lay on top of him, not scrambling off as I used my body to shield my movements.

"What are you doing?" growled the Shrouded Mage, stepping toward us. He seemed to think I'd gone mad with terror and attempted to escape, colliding with Zak in the process.

My hand slipped inside Zak's jacket, my fingers feeling for the first pocket. Last time, Zak had told me to reach past the first pocket to the second, and I could think of only one type of composition he would want in easier reach than a healing one.

Pulling out the wad of parchments I found inside—each one a tiny roll—I ripped one at random.

I couldn't tell if anything had happened, but the Shrouded Mage bellowed wordlessly and leaped toward us.

I didn't bother wasting time reading any of the others. I just ripped the next one. And the next. Still nothing happened that I could see, but the masked man in front of us bellowed again.

I kept going, ripping every parchment the pocket had contained. If I was right, and they were shields, then we were now cocooned in every protection Zak had in his arsenal. There was still a risk to me. Zak might have written them to protect only himself. But I didn't feel afraid. I knew Zak, and he had too much compassion to think only of himself in crafting his shields. If a sudden disaster befell him, he would want to shield everyone in his radius, regardless of their status.

The Shrouded Mage tried to reach for me, but he bounced back as if he'd encountered an invisible wall. He glared at me, the force of his eyes suffocating as he reached into his own jacket.

I gulped and plunged my hand back toward Zak's pockets. I pulled out parchments as quickly as I could, emptying his various pockets, but this time I took the time to read them.

The Shrouded Mage ripped a parchment, and I glanced up, but nothing happened. He growled and pulled out another one as I turned back to the parchments in my hands. Zak was a Callinos. He was strong. His shields would hold.

They had to.

Again and again, I plunged my hand back into Zak's jacket as the mage only steps away from us ripped a second, third, and fourth parchment. Finally, my desperately skimming eyes found the words I was looking for.

I ripped the paper, still half-sprawled across Zak's still body, flicking my fingers awkwardly toward him. He moved beneath me, pushing me gently aside and springing to his feet. His full attention was locked on the mage who stood feet away from us, another parchment in his hands.

Faster than seemed possible, Zak's hand flashed into his jacket and reappeared with a fresh composition. He didn't need to look at it, tearing it confidently and watching his opponent.

For a moment the Shrouded Mage looked fearful. But when nothing discernible happened, he grinned.

"You're going to need more strength than that," he taunted, and I realized he must have worked a shield of his own at some point, the power of it strong enough to beat back whatever power Zak had sent at him.

Zak didn't respond, merely plunging his hand back into his jacket and emerging with two more parchments. The Shrouded Mage also lunged for another composition, but

Zak was faster. Our attacker's hands froze, an untorn parchment clasped uselessly between his fingers.

His eyes rolled wildly in his head, but they seemed to be the only part of him he could move. I gave a gasping sob of a breath, and Zak turned instantly to look down at me where I still sat on the cobblestones beside him.

"Are you hurt?" He pulled me up, examining me from head to foot. His frown landed on the scraped and bloodied skin on the back of my hands.

"You protected me," he murmured softly, so much love in his voice that it hurt.

He pulled me toward him, and I sank against his chest, my whole body trembling with the aftereffects of our desperate struggle.

"You saved us," he murmured into my hair. "I was so afraid for you, but you were magnificent."

I laughed shakily. "They were your compositions."

"But I was helpless to make use of them without you." I could hear the smile in his voice. "We make a good team."

I drew a shuddering breath. "I'm sorry I used all your shields. I didn't have time to read them and pick the right ones, plus I didn't know how strong they were."

"You did the right thing," he said immediately. "I can replenish shields." He pulled back to look at me. "But how did you know that I would even have shields or where to find them?"

I explained my reasoning, and he shook his head. "Your mind never ceases to amaze me."

I glanced uneasily at the Shrouded Mage, unable to relax while he stood so close to us, even if he was bound. "How long will your binding power last?"

"Long enough," Zak said grimly. "My first one burned out against his shield, but it burned most of the power of the shield in the process. So I worked two more. He'll be held that way for hours unless someone releases him."

A deadly smile flashed over his face. "I don't think he expected me to have more than one binding composition. But I was an Academy trainee only months ago. I'm fresh from endless mock battles in the arena."

"I don't want to wait around here for hours," I said. "Even if it is safe."

"Definitely not." Zak's fingers already reached for another composition.

He took longer making his choice this time, finally selecting two. He ripped them both without offering an explanation, pulling me back into his arms and holding me tight, as if to reassure himself I really was still in one piece. I accepted his embrace without comment, needing the reassurance myself.

Barely two minutes had passed, however, when pounding feet sounded and two guards burst into the alley. Zak stepped calmly away from me.

"Thank you for coming so quickly." He nodded at the men.

"We followed your composition," one of the two commonborns said, admiration in his eyes. "A neat working, that one."

Zak smiled. "Thank you. It's my own design."

"What's going on here?" the second guard asked, having stepped into the alley far enough to see the man frozen in place behind us. The guard's eyes widened as he took in the

material wrapped around the man's head and his volumi-
nous cloak.

He exchanged a look with his companion. "Don't tell
me this is…"

"I think your mages will find it is, indeed, the Shrouded
Killer," Zak said. "He just attacked me, but thankfully Aria
and I were able to overcome him. I've sent a second
composition to the closest law enforcement hub to request
backup for you, and I've instructed them to come with at
least two mages."

"That's all right, then," the second guard said. "The
mages will sort it out." He looked relieved that he wasn't
going to be asked to take charge of the infamous serial
killer himself.

"It doesn't fit the profile." A hint of skepticism
sounded in the first guard's voice, despite his respectful
tone. "You're not a commonborn. And this isn't the lower
city."

I cleared my throat, willing my voice not to shake as I
took a half step forward. "I think I might be able to explain
that."

All three men looked at me curiously.

"When he first arrived, he said that he'd heard Zak has
been looking for him."

"Looking for him?" The first guard's brows rose almost
to his hairline. "And what reason would you have to do
that, My Lord? You've a black robe not a red one."

Zak shifted uncomfortably.

"He thought the mages should have been doing more to
find him," I said, not sharing his discomfort. We were
talking to commonborns, and I suspected the common-

born law enforcement guards had been feeling even more frustration with their superiors than Zak had been.

The two men exchanged a look but neither of them protested.

"He wasn't actually looking for him, not actively." I bit my lip. "I think it was my fault."

Zak frowned. "What are you talking about?"

"The last day we spoke in the lower city, I thought I saw someone nearby, close enough to hear us. I was just embarrassed, of course I never dreamed…" I winced. "But I guess after all those times wandering around back alleys, we finally did stumble on the Shrouded Mage. And I was talking in an exaggerated way, telling you to stop hunting the Shrouded Killer."

Zak's eyes widened. "And you made me promise to stay out of the lower city after that."

"Thank goodness I did!" I shuddered to think what would have happened if the killer had caught Zak alone.

"We mentioned starting at the University as well," Zak said. "And this is the first day of classes. He must have been lurking outside the University waiting for me to appear."

"You're fortunate to have escaped," one of the guards said with a low whistle.

"It was all because of Aria." Zak smiled at me proudly.

"He underestimated me," I said quietly. "I'm a common-born, so he just dismissed me. I don't think it even occurred to him that I might be a threat."

The tramp of more hurrying feet sounded, along with a shout, calling for the traffic on the street to make way. We all turned toward the alley mouth in time to be greeted by a wave of red.

Zak stepped up to the mage in charge of the squad, engaging him in hurried conversation. The man exclaimed, clapping Zak on the shoulder, and the prisoner was soon taken in hand by the red-robed mages. They worked a number of compositions I couldn't see or feel before dismantling Zak's binding and marching the man away.

He tried to growl at us as he passed, but one of the mages yanked him viciously forward.

"Don't worry," the other mage said to us. "He won't be bothering you again."

They took the rest of the guards with them, including the first two, and the crowd that had started to gather streamed up the street in their wake. Finally only Zak and I remained. He took my hand, trying to gently tug me toward the street.

"I'm going to walk you home," he said firmly, clearly unwilling to accept any arguments on the matter.

I stood my ground, however, tugging back until he stopped. He looked inquiringly at me, and I took a deep breath.

"Did you mean everything you said?" I asked him.

"About you saving us?" He stepped to my side. "Of course."

"No, earlier. This morning."

Hope blazed in his eyes. "Every word."

I took another deep breath. "Then I'm willing to try. I'll fight at your side for a future where we can be together."

He didn't ask any questions, merely sweeping me into his arms and kissing me until we were both so breathless we fell apart.

Smiling down at me, he finally asked. "What made you

change your mind? Was it the heroics I displayed by lying on the ground like a motionless board while a maniac tried to kill us?"

I laughed but quickly sobered. "I'll admit that my fear for you made a few things clear to me. If I'm willing to die for you, why would I walk away without even fighting for us?"

His arms tightened, and he looked like he was going to kiss me again, but I held him off. "But it was also the Shrouded Mage himself."

"Do I make a dashing comparison? I'm glad to know I rate at least a little higher than a serial killer."

I whacked him lightly. "I'm being serious. Did you see the way he looked at me? I'm not surprised he's been killing people in the lower city. He's not like other mages. They think they're above commonborn, but they still see them as human. But the Shrouded Mage..." I shuddered. "I don't think he sees commonborns as people at all."

Zak frowned, his arms once again tightening around me.

"It made me realize that he's not the only one who sees commonborns differently from most mages," I continued. "You don't see us the same way other mages do either. You see us as equals. And it's not just me. You were like that before you ever met me."

"You're right, I do," he said. "And I hope that one day more mages will think the same way. It may take decades— even generations—but I believe things will change."

"And that," I said with a smile, "is one of the many reasons I love you."

This time I didn't push him away when he leaned down to kiss me again.

EPILOGUE

My parents proved as willing to embrace Zak as I had predicted, their opinion changing instantly once they understood he meant to defy his entire society for my sake. Or it might have been his role in saving me from the Shrouded Mage. He tried to tell them I had been the one to save him, but my mother merely collapsed sobbing on his shoulder, thanking him again and again for saving her baby.

Zak's parents proved less amenable. He seemed undaunted by their opposition, but I was less able to believe they would eventually come around.

Those doubts filled my mind as I moped at home on the next rest day. I was brooding over the future when my mother called that I had a visitor. My mood lifted immediately, given the enthusiasm in her voice, and I hurried toward the door, expecting to see Zak.

Instead, I found Faylee.

"Welcome back!" I exclaimed, almost as glad to see her as I would have been to see Zak.

She didn't waste any time on greetings, however, thrusting an armful of material toward me.

"Quick, go and put that on. As fast as you can. We need to get going."

"What?" I stared at her in confusion.

But my mother flapped her arms at me, gesturing for me to take the clothing Faylee was holding out. "You heard her! Hurry!"

Bemused, I accepted the gown being pushed on me and raced back to my room. I pulled it on with some difficulty, gaping at myself in the mirror when I'd finished.

I smoothed my hands down the soft material, finer than anything I'd ever worn. It looked like something Gina's mother would put her in—right before complaining that the sash had been tied crooked. Clearly it had come from the Robarts' wardrobes. But why was I being hurried into it?

When I reappeared, Faylee ran a critical eye over me.

"Thank goodness it's the right length," she said. "I wasn't sure. Now come on, we need to get going."

"But where? And why the hurry?" I threw a helpless look at my mother as Faylee hustled me out the door and onto the street.

A carriage waited for us, barely able to fit on our narrow street. I only had time to raise my brows before I was thrust up the steps and inside.

Once we were both seated and the horses had begun moving, I tried again.

"Whatever is going on, Faylee? Where are we going?"

"To the palace," she said matter-of-factly. "To see the king. I was delayed because I had to find a relative the same height and build as you, and we don't want to be late."

"The king?" My mouth fell open, terror filling me. "Faylee, why are we going to see the king?"

"Mainly you're going to see him. I'm just tagging along because I have enough credit to force myself into situations where I'm not wanted." She flashed her straight, white teeth in a grin.

"It would have been your young man here with you instead of me," she continued at my unintelligible sound of protest. "But thankfully he has the good sense to recognize his own limitations—such as the last-minute provision of an appropriate gown. So he trusted me with getting you to the palace on time. And I believe in keeping the trust given to me."

"But why does the king want to see me?" I managed to get out.

"You must have heard that the Reds confirmed the man you captured is the real Shrouded Mage," she said. "And they rushed through his sealing ceremony only yesterday."

I nodded. The lower city had been abuzz.

"They're still debating what to do with him next—whether to execute him or just lock him away for life," she continued. "But as far as the king is concerned, this chapter is closed, and he's very pleased about it." She looked grim despite her words, and I cast her a careful look, remembering something important.

"I heard the last victim was a Robart," I said. "I'm sorry for your loss."

She nodded. "He was a distant cousin, but the family is furious."

"Is that why you're here?" I asked.

She nodded. "The crown allowed law enforcement to deceive the commonborn population, so that we thought the threat was over. I'm sure the king was less than pleased when he heard the next victim came from a family with teeth." She bared hers, her expression fierce.

"But he's the king!" I protested.

Faylee looked at me and laughed, her expression relaxing. "Calm down. I'm not going to challenge him for his throne. I'm just going to do the same thing anyone with power would do in my place—remind him that I can't be safely ignored and see if I can maneuver the situation to some advantage." She gave me a smile. "In this case, I intend to right my family's ledger by settling an old wrong."

I decided not to even question that, instead looking out the closest window as the University flashed past. If we'd already reached the University, we were almost at the palace.

I gulped as the carriage rolled through the open palace gates. I wasn't sure my legs were going to hold me as I climbed down, but thankfully Zak was waiting for me, taking my arm and giving me strength.

I smiled up at him, but my eyes must have looked a little wild because he laughed quietly.

"Relax. We're here to be commended, not punished."

I nodded, refraining from reminding him how different our situations were. He had probably attended functions at the palace since he was a small child, whereas I had never even dreamed of stepping inside the palace grounds. It was only a reminder of the differences between us at a time when I'd resolved to stop thinking of them as much as possible.

All too quickly, we were swept up the grand steps of the palace by waiting footmen and ushered through a bewildering set of corridors. Everywhere I saw white marble, red and gold decorations softening the severity of the stone.

I was still trying to take it all in when a footman opened a door and announced us.

"Zakary of Callinos and Aria of Corrin."

Zakary swept inside, taking me with him, and Faylee trailed in behind us. "And Faylee, also of Corrin," she said with a cheeky grin that stopped just short of disrespect.

"Faylee," a young woman said, clearly stifling a laugh. "It's always lovely to see you."

"And you, Princess Elena." Faylee grinned back, giving a small curtsy.

I dropped into a curtsy of my own, swallowing as I realized I faced not only King Stellan, but also Queen Verena, Crown Princess Lucienne, Prince Lucas, and the Spoken Mage, a small baby girl in her arms. The entire royal family was there—with the exception of the toddler prince.

When I rose, I was relieved to see that everyone present was smiling at us, with the exception of Lucas. But his attention was on his wife and baby, so I didn't think it indicated his disapproval.

"We understand extraordinary thanks are in order." The queen spoke in a deep, musical voice.

"You succeeded where the entire law enforcement discipline could not," King Stellan added. "Duke Soren is shown up." He sounded amused rather than annoyed by our outshining the Head of Law Enforcement.

Zak gave another bow, and I quickly dropped into a second curtsy.

"We are pleased to serve Corrin in any way we can," he said with a smile. "Even if that's by being attacked."

"You were more than just a victim," the Spoken Mage said, "and I understand you worked together to overcome him." She turned her gaze on me, her brow creasing slightly. "But I know you!" she exclaimed, and I squeaked. "We met at the sealing ceremony at the start of summer. You're the one with all the brothers. Four!"

She laughed, throwing a speaking glance at Prince Lucas that I didn't even try to understand.

"Three is quite enough," he said to her in a low aside, and she laughed again before turning back to me.

"But I had no idea you were so heroic."

"They were Zak's compositions," I managed to say, amazed my voice still worked. "But he was incapacitated, so I had to work them."

"Once again we see what can be accomplished when mages and commonborns work together in partnership." Her words were light, but I could sense they weren't idle. There were undercurrents in the room that I was far from understanding.

"And you have both only just graduated from your respective schools," Prince Lucas said, giving us his attention for the first time. "It was a truly remarkable feat. You must tell us how we can reward you."

His father shifted slightly, and I wondered if the talk of a reward was unexpected to the king. I had no idea what sort of reward the prince had in mind, and I certainly wasn't going to risk opening my mouth and making a suggestion.

Zak, however, showed no such compunction.

"The only reward we seek is your blessing on our betrothal." He met the king's eyes boldly.

The various reactions on the faces of the royals were subtle, but they must have been greatly shocked to show any reaction at all. Only the Spoken Mage and Prince Lucas didn't reveal the slightest hint of surprise.

The king cast a swift look at them both, but when he spoke, it was to Zak. "I didn't realize you were a couple."

"Aria has only just agreed to marry me," Zak said. "So it isn't widely known. But we are aware that many will oppose the match—my own parents among them. Your blessing would go a long way toward ensuring our happy future."

The king cleared his throat, glancing at his wife.

"You have made an unusual choice, Zakary of Callinos." The queen sounded neither approving nor disapproving.

"Perhaps," Zak said. "But not a surprising one, I think. Aria is beautiful, intelligent, and fierce. If she could control power, every mageborn at the Academy would have wanted to either befriend her or marry her."

The crown princess let out a sudden chuckle. "That I can believe."

"You give no thought to your children?" the queen asked, making me flush and duck my head.

"I believe the common assumptions on that matter to be wrong, Your Majesty," Zak said respectfully, but with confidence. "I fully expect my children to equal my strength, although of course the status of their mother will prevent their surpassing it. I believe, however, that they will gain other attributes from her that will be worth any small sacrifice on that front."

"A gamble," the king said in something almost like a grumble.

"It will take twenty years to prove I'm right on this issue, but I am content to wait that long." Zak looked sideways at me, his gaze warm. "I expect them to be a most joyous twenty years."

"Well said!" the Spoken Mage murmured.

Faylee stepped forward, having lurked in the background for so long that I had nearly forgotten her presence.

"I know the Robarts would welcome it, were you to bestow your royal approval on this union," she said in a formal voice that made me eye her with concern. She sounded nothing like herself.

But when I took in her expression and manner, I realized she wasn't speaking as herself. She was speaking on behalf of her powerful and wealthy merchant family, not as a single individual.

She continued on, strength in her voice. "We welcome the changing attitude toward commonborns in Ardann, even as we grieve our recent loss. It would bring us comfort in our grief to know that the crown supports those mages who begin to see your commonborn subjects differently." She stepped back, and I waited with bated breath.

Still the king hesitated, glancing toward the queen.

It was Crown Princess Lucienne who stepped forward,

speaking in her father's place. "The crown welcomes young love wherever it is freely given." She gave Zak and me a warm smile. "Of course we would be delighted to bless your union."

The king let out a breath and nodded his head. He might have been less ready than the younger generation to embrace change, but he didn't mean to gainsay his daughter and heir. Perhaps the rumors about his ill health were true. Along with those that said the crown princess had been taking on more responsibilities of late.

Zak bowed again, giving his thanks on behalf of us both, and to my relief I quickly found myself back outside the door. Only when it closed behind us, shutting us off from the royal family, did I take an easy breath.

"Did that really happen?" I asked in a daze.

"It did!" Zak looked exultant. "My parents won't dare oppose us now." He turned to Faylee. "Thank you, Faylee."

"Robarts pay our debts," she said with a smile. "As I have made clear to my family." From her fierce expression I wondered if it wasn't only the royals who were in the middle of a gradual handover of power.

I stiffened as the door opened behind us, but thankfully there was no sign of the king. The room beyond the door looked empty, so the royals must have left through another entrance. Only the Spoken Mage remained in the doorway, the baby princess still in her arms.

She gave Zak a conspiratorial smile. "That went exceptionally well." She spoke quietly but with conviction. "I wasn't sure if Lucienne would speak up for us."

I blinked at her. The Spoken Mage had conspired with Zak to orchestrate that scene? That seemed to confirm that

Prince Lucas had surprised the king with his suggestion of a reward.

Princess Elena smiled at me. "I'm determined that I won't be the only commonborn to benefit from a change in social status. You have managed to win one of the best among the mageborn in Zakary, and I have high hopes that you will do much for the commonborn cause in the future —by your existence alone, although I'm sure your contribution won't end there."

"Th…Thank you, Your Highness," I managed, stumbling over my words.

"And if Zakary proves right," she said, "we could yet change Ardann's fate."

"You think it's possible, then?" Faylee asked.

"His reasoning is sound." Elena looked thoughtful. "Let us consider it an investment for the future. It will take time before we can be certain, but I have hope that future generations will live very different lives from those of the past."

"Let us hope so, indeed, Your Highness." Faylee and the princess exchanged smiles.

"Zak has ideas about how the commonborn could be benefited now," I blurted out, startled by my own daring.

But Princess Elena looked intrigued as she smiled from me to Zak. "Does he? I would be most glad to hear them some time. You must come and drink tea with Prince Lucas and me before your wedding, Zakary, so we can hear all about these ideas."

Zak flushed with pleasure, bowing low. I took his arm, filled with pride, although I still didn't understand everything that had just occurred.

I refrained from any questions, however, waiting until

we'd bidden the Spoken Mage farewell, and the three of us were safely back inside Faylee's carriage.

"I don't understand," I said, as the carriage rumbled off. "What was all that about changing the future?"

Zak grinned. "I thought my theory might get the Spoken Mage's attention, and I was right. If I'm proved correct, it upends the established thinking about the best ways to preserve bloodlines of power."

I blinked. "What?"

"If a powerful mage can marry a commonborn and his or her children will equal the power of the mage parent, then the crown should be encouraging mages to look to the commonborn population for romantic partners. We could increase the total number of mages exponentially within only a few generations."

I gaped at him. "But—"

"Oh, the royals won't do it themselves," he said with a laugh. "The crown must preserve its power. And there will always be couples among the mages, that's inevitable. But if we can increase the number of mage bloodlines proportional to the general population—if we can regain the numbers Ardann used to have before the old wars decimated the mage population…"

Faylee leaned forward to grin at me. "We could be like the Sekali Empire, who never lost their original mage numbers."

"You mean, everyone could be sealed as toddlers, like the Sekalis are?" I asked, not quite comprehending the enormity of what she was suggesting.

Faylee leaned back again, but her smile was one of satisfaction. "As Elena said, it's not something that will happen all at once. But there is hope for the future." She winked at me. "And profit to be made for those at the forefront of history."

I shook my head, laughing in spite of myself. Of course Faylee had acted on my behalf for more reasons than one. It was no wonder people predicted she would be head of the Robarts before many more years had passed.

"But that's all for the future." Zak took my hand. "The important thing for now is that our betrothal has royal approval."

He swayed toward me, but Faylee cleared her throat loudly, and he pulled back, glancing at her and chuckling.

"I confess there are a few more matters in the here and now that still interest me," she said. "And I suspect Aria might be interested in at least one of them as well."

I turned a questioning gaze on her, and she grinned, an expression that looked more predatory than amused. "I thought you might like to know that Teacher Wendell will never be receiving a job offer from the Robarts. He is entirely unsuitable—and untrustworthy besides."

I nodded, part of me relieved to hear that his misuse of his position wasn't going to be rewarded. But that meant he would remain in his current role, and I couldn't help feeling bad for his students.

"I'm glad to hear he won't receive a lucrative job offer," Zak said grimly, clearly suffering no mixed feelings. "And I intend to make sure he doesn't remain a teacher, either. He cannot be allowed to hold power over the future of any more young people."

I squeezed his hand. "Thank you," I murmured, my heart full. I hadn't even needed to voice my concerns. Zak already shared them without needing any prompting from me.

He responded to the soft note in my voice, turning to me with a light in his eyes. "Will you agree to set a date for the wedding now?" His expression turned wheedling. "It can be as far away as you like, but I want to know how many days I need to count down."

I laughed and slid against his side, tucking myself against his shoulder.

"Let me think," I said in mock consideration, winking at Faylee on the other side of the carriage. "Perhaps the day after we graduate from the University? That's only four years away."

"Four years!" he cried in horror, and Faylee and I both broke into laughter.

"Very well, then," I said in mock surrender when we regained control. "Perhaps we can set an earlier date."

Zak gave a laugh of his own and dropped a kiss on the top of my head. "How about a midwinter wedding? I've heard those are lovely."

I considered the idea, a grin spreading over my face. "That sounds perfect."

Zak gazed down at me, so much love in his face that Faylee sighed.

"I'm still here," she said, setting Zak and I off into a fresh round of laughter.

I wasn't sure I was going to stop laughing with joy and delight for a long time to come. I had never imagined that my future could so far surpass the dreams I had worked so hard for. But with Zak at my side, I knew that we would fulfill every hope the Spoken Mage placed in us.

To find out what happens to the next generation, and to explore the re-discovery of energy mages, read my Hidden Mage series, starting with Crown of Secrets, when Elena's daughter is sent to the Kallorwegian Academy.

To be informed of future releases, as well as Spoken Mage bonus shorts, please sign up to my mailing list at www.melaniecellier.com. You'll find an exclusive bonus chapter of Voice of Power—retold from Lucas's point of view—in the welcome email, as well as several other bonus chapters freely available on my website.

And if you enjoyed my Spoken Mage series, please spread the word and help other readers find it! You could start by leaving a review on Amazon or Goodreads or Facebook or any other social media site. Your review would be very much appreciated and would make a big difference!

ACKNOWLEDGMENTS

For some years, I had no particular intention of returning to my Spoken Mage world. After writing two full series in it, plus a companion novel, I had moved on to other story worlds. But one day I had the thought of writing a Spoken Mage short story, and that thought grew until it became this novella. And it turned out that I greatly enjoyed returning to the world of Ardann and the power of written words. So much so, in fact, that I suspect there will be more Spoken Mage novellas to come. There is something particularly enjoyable about exploring different corners of this story world without the pressure of a full series, and knowing that I'm writing for readers who are already familiar with the world.

Over the last decade, I've written a great many acknowledgments. Again and again, I've thanked my beta readers, my editors, my cover designer, my map artist, my narrators, my family, and always God. And every time it's been true. It's still true. My team is amazing, and I'm incredibly grateful to have them. And I'm even more grateful to have been created—and to continue to be loved —as a creative being. But this time I want to focus on a different acknowledgment.

As I return to the Spoken Mage world, I want to focus on acknowledging you, my reader. I'm so grateful to the people who have read, loved, and even been inspired by the Spoken Mage books. If you were interested enough in Elena's adventures to have made it through a companion novel and now a novella, I want to thank you from the bottom of my heart. I appreciate you more than I can say.

I hope my books are a positive in your life, however small, and I want to take this chance to let you know that you are a positive in my life. Sometimes, when something about the writing journey is sitting particularly heavily, I think back to memorable communications from readers—emails or comments from people who connected with my characters and stories and wanted to thank me for writing them. You aren't speaking into a void! And even if all you do is continue to purchase or borrow my books and read them, you're making a difference to me. Thank you!

ABOUT THE AUTHOR

Melanie Cellier grew up on a staple diet of books, books and more books. And although she got older, she never stopped loving children's and young adult novels.

She always wanted to write one herself, but it took three careers and three different continents before she actually managed it.

She now feels incredibly fortunate to spend her time writing from her home in Adelaide, Australia where she keeps an eye out for koalas in her backyard. Her staple diet hasn't changed much, although she's added choc mint Rooibos tea and Chicken Crimpies to the list.

She writes young adult fantasy including books in her *Spoken Mage* world, her *Mage's Influence* world, and her various *Four Kingdoms* and *Kingdoms of Legacy* series that are made up of linked stand-alone stories that retell classic fairy tales.

www.ingramcontent.com/pod-product-compliance
Lightning Source LLC
Chambersburg PA
CBHW022051050726
47591CB00002B/494